the
thing
about
jellyfish

the
thing
about
jellyfish

ali benjamin

LB

LITTLE, BROWN AND COMPANY
New York · Boston

Little, Brown and Company

Hachette Book Group
1290 Avenue of the Americas, New York, NY 10104
Visit us at lb-kids.com

Little, Brown and Company is a division of Hachette Book Group, Inc.
The Little, Brown name and logo are trademarks of Hachette Book Group, Inc.

The publisher is not responsible for websites (or their content) that are not owned by the publisher.

First Edition: September 2015
First International Edition: September 2015

Library of Congress Cataloging-in-Publication Data

Benjamin, Ali.
 The thing about jellyfish / by Ali Benjamin.—First edition.
  pages cm
 Summary: Twelve-year-old Suzy Swanson wades through her intense grief over the loss of her best friend by investigating the rare jellyfish she is convinced was responsible for her friend's death.
  ISBN 978-0-316-38086-7 (hardcover)—ISBN 978-0-316-38083-6 (ebook)—ISBN 978-0-316-34946-8 (international) [1. Grief—Fiction. 2. Best friends—Fiction. 3. Friendship—Fiction. 4. Jellyfishes—Fiction.] I. Title.
 PZ7.1.B453Th 2015
 [E]—dc23
                                                                    2014044025

10 9 7 6 5 4 2 1

RRD-C

Printed in the United States of America

for curious kids
everywhere

ghost heart

A JELLYFISH, IF YOU WATCH IT LONG ENOUGH, begins to look like a heart beating. It doesn't matter what kind: the blood-red *Atolla* with its flashing siren lights, the frilly flower hat variety, or the near-transparent moon jelly, *Aurelia aurita*. It's their pulse, the way they contract swiftly, then release. Like a ghost heart—a heart you can see right through, right into some other world where everything you ever lost has gone to hide.

Jellyfish don't even have hearts, of course—no heart, no brain, no bone, no blood. But watch them for a while. You will see them beating.

Mrs. Turton says that if you lived to be eighty years old, your heart would beat three billion times. I was thinking about that, trying to imagine a number that large. Three *billion*. Count back three billion hours, and modern humans don't exist—just wild-eyed cave people, all hairy and grunting. Three billion years, and life itself barely exists. And yet here's your heart, doing its job all the time, one beat after the next, all the way up to three billion.

But only if you get to live that long.

It's beating when you're sleeping, when you're watching TV, when you're standing at the beach with your toes in the sand. Maybe while you're standing there, you're looking at sparkles of white light on dark ocean, wondering if it's worth getting your hair wet again. Maybe you notice that your bathing suit straps are just a little too tight on your sunburned shoulders or that the sun is too bright in your eyes.

You squint a little. You are as alive as anybody else right now.

Meanwhile, the waves keep rolling over your toes, one after another (like a heartbeat, almost—you can notice or not), and the elastic is digging in, and perhaps what you notice, more than the sun or the straps, is how cold the water is, or the way the waves create hollow places in the wet sand beneath your feet. Your mom is off at your side somewhere; she's taking a picture, and you know you should turn to her and smile.

But you don't. You don't turn, you don't smile, you just keep looking out at the sea, and neither of you knows what matters about this moment, or what's about to happen (how could you?).

And the whole while, your heart just keeps going. It does what it needs to do, one beat after another, until it gets the message that it's time to stop, which might happen a few minutes from now, and you don't even know it.

Because some hearts beat only about 412 million times.

Which might sound like a lot. But the truth is, it barely even gets you twelve years.

part one

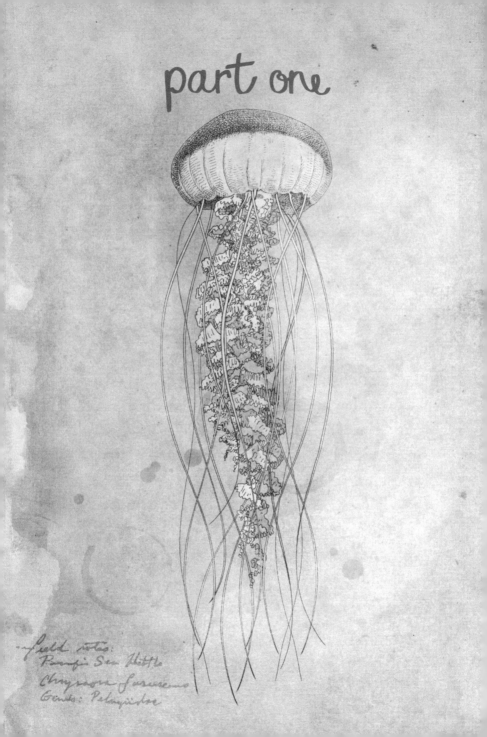

field notes:
Pacific Sea Nettle
Chrysaora fuscescens
Genus: Pelagiidae

Purpose

It doesn't matter if you're writing a middle school lab report or a real scientific paper. Begin with an introduction that establishes the purpose for all the information that's to follow. What do we hope to find out from this research? How does it relate to human concerns?

—Mrs. Turton, Grade 7 Life Science teacher
Eugene Field Memorial Middle School,
South Grove, Massachusetts

touch

DURING THE FIRST THREE WEEKS OF SEVENTH grade, I'd learned one thing above all else: A person can become invisible simply by staying quiet.

I'd always thought that being seen was about what people perceived with their eyes. But by the time the Eugene Field Memorial Middle School made the fall trip to the aquarium, I, Suzy Swanson, had disappeared entirely. Being seen is more about the ears than the eyes, it turns out.

We were standing in the touch tank room, listening to a bearded aquarium worker speak into a microphone. "Hold your hand flat," he said. He explained that if we placed our hands in the tank and held them perfectly still, tiny sharks and rays would graze against our palms like friendly house cats. "They'll come to you, but you have to keep your hand flat and very still."

I would have liked to feel a shark against my fingers. But it was too crowded at the tank, too noisy. I stood in the back of the room. Just watching.

We had made tie-dye shirts in art class in preparation for this field trip. We'd stained our hands neon orange and blue, and now we wore the shirts like a psychedelic uniform. I guess the idea was that we'd be easy to spot if any of us got lost. A few of the pretty girls—girls like Aubrey LaValley and Molly Sampson and Jenna Van Hoose—had tied their T-shirts into knots at their hips. Mine hung over my jeans like an old art smock.

It was exactly one month since the Worst Thing had happened, and almost as long since I'd started *not-talking*. Which isn't refusing to talk, like everyone thinks it is. It's just deciding not to fill the world with words if you don't have to. It is the opposite of *constant-talking*, which is what I used to do, and it's better than *small talk*, which is what people wished I did.

If I made small talk, maybe my parents wouldn't insist that I see *the kind of doctor you can talk to*, which is what I would be doing this afternoon, after today's field trip. Frankly, their reasoning didn't make sense. I mean, if a person isn't talking—if that's the whole point—then maybe *the kind of doctor you can talk to* is the very last person you should have to see.

Besides, I knew what *the kind of doctor you can talk to* meant. It meant my parents thought I had problems with my brain, and not the kind of problems that made it hard to do math or learn to read. It meant they thought I had mental problems, the kind that Franny would have called *cray cray*, which is short for *crazy*, which comes from the word *craze*, which means "to fill with cracks and flaws."

It meant I had cracks and flaws.

"Keep your hands flat," said the aquarium worker to no one in particular—which was fine, because nobody was listening to him anyway. "These animals can actually feel heartbeats in the room. You really don't need to wiggle your fingers."

Justin Maloney, who is a boy who still moves his lips when he reads, kept trying to grab the rays' tails. His pants were so loose that every time he leaned over the water, I could see several inches of his underwear. I noticed his tie-dye was inside out. Another ray passed, and Justin reached in so fast that he splashed water all over Sarah Johnston, the new girl, who was standing next to him. Sarah wiped the salt water off her forehead and moved a few steps away from Justin.

Sarah is very quiet, which I like, and she smiled at me on the first day of school. But then Molly walked over and started talking to her, and then I saw her talking to Aubrey at the lockers, and now Sarah's shirt was knotted at the waist, just like theirs.

I pushed a clump of hair out of my eyes and tried to tuck it behind my ears—*Mizz Frizz, hair so impossible*. It immediately fell back in my face again.

Dylan Parker snuck up behind Aubrey. He

grabbed her shoulders and shook them. "Shark!" he shouted.

The boys around him laughed. Aubrey squealed, and so did all the girls around her, but they were all giggling in that way that girls sometimes do around boys.

And of course that made me think of Franny. Because if she had been there, she would have been giggling, too.

I felt that sweaty-sick feeling then, the same thing I felt whenever I thought about Franny.

I squeezed my eyes shut. For a few seconds, the darkness was a relief. But then a picture popped into my head, and it was not a good one. I imagined the touch tank breaking, the rays and tiny sharks spilling out all over the floor. And that made me wonder how long the animals could last before they drowned in the open air.

Everything would feel cold and shrill and bright to them. And then the animals would stop breathing forever.

I opened my eyes.

Sometimes you want things to change so badly, you can't even stand to be in the same room with the way things actually are.

In a far corner, an arrow pointed down a staircase to another exhibit, JELLIES, on the floor below. I walked over to the stairs, then glanced back to see if anyone would notice. Dylan flicked water at Aubrey, who squealed again. One of the chaperones walked toward them, already scolding.

Even in my neon tie-dye, even with my *Mizz Frizz* hair, nobody seemed to see me.

I walked down the stairs, toward the JELLIES exhibit.

No one noticed. No one at all.

sometimes things just happen

YOU WERE DEAD FOR TWO WHOLE DAYS BEFORE *I even knew.*

It was afternoon, late August, the end of the long, lonely summer after sixth grade. My mom called me in from outside, and I knew something was wrong—really, really wrong—just by looking at her. I got scared then, thinking that maybe something had happened to my dad. But since the divorce, would it even matter to my mom if he got hurt? Then I thought maybe something was wrong with my brother.

"Zu," *Mom started. I heard the refrigerator hum, a* poink poink *from the shower dripping, the ticking that* comes from the old clock on the mantel whose time is always wrong unless I remember to wind it.

Long streaks of sun crossed through the window, like spirits through walls. They lay down on the carpet and were still.

Mom spoke evenly, her words coming out at normal speed, yet everything seemed slowed down, as if time itself had grown heavy. Or maybe like time had stopped existing altogether.

"Franny Jackson drowned."

Three words. They probably took only a couple of seconds to come out, but they seemed to last about half an hour.

My first thought was: That's weird. Why is she using Franny's last name? *I couldn't remember my mom ever using your last name. You were always just Franny to her.*

And then I realized the thing she'd said after she said your name.

Drowned.

She said you had drowned.

"She was on vacation," Mom continued. I noticed

how perfectly still she was sitting, how rigid her shoulders were. "A beach vacation."

Then she added, as if it would somehow help the thing she'd said make any sense at all, "In Maryland."

But of course her words didn't make sense.

There were a million reasons they didn't. They didn't make sense because it hadn't been that long since I'd seen you, and you were as alive as anyone then. Her words didn't make sense because you were always such a good swimmer, better than I was from the instant we met.

They didn't make sense because the way things ended between us was not the way they were supposed to end. They were not the way anything should ever end.

And yet here was my mom, she was right in front of me, and she was saying these words. And if her words were true, if she was right about this thing she was telling me, it meant that the last glimpse I'd had of you— walking down the hallway on the last day of sixth grade, carrying those bags of wet clothes and crying—would be the final one I'd ever have.

I stared at my mom. "No, she didn't," I said.

You hadn't. You couldn't have. I was sure of that.

Mom opened her mouth to say something, then closed it again.

"She didn't," I insisted, louder this time.

"It was Tuesday," Mom said. Her voice was quieter than before, as if my getting louder had sucked the strength from her own breath. "It happened on Tuesday. I only just found out."

It was Thursday now.

Two whole days had gone by.

Whenever I think about those two days—about the space between you ending and me knowing—I think about the stars. Did you know that the light from our nearest star takes four years to reach us? Which means when we see it—when we see any star—we are really seeing what it looked like in the past. All those twinkling lights, every star in the sky, could have burned out years ago—the entire night sky could be empty this very minute, and we wouldn't even know it.

"She could swim," I said. "She was a good swimmer, remember?"

When Mom said nothing, I tried again. "Remember, Mom?"

Mom just closed her eyes and placed her forehead in the palms of her hands.

"It's impossible," I insisted. Why couldn't she see how impossible this was?

When Mom looked up, she spoke slowly, like she was trying really hard to make sure I heard every single word. "Even good swimmers can drown, Zu."

"But it doesn't make sense. How could she—?"

"Not everything makes sense, Zu. Sometimes things just happen." She shook her head and took a deep breath. "This probably doesn't even seem real. It doesn't seem real to me, either."

Then she closed her eyes for a few long seconds. When she opened them again, her face twisted up in a terrible way. Tears began spilling down her cheeks. "I'm sorry," she said. "I'm just so sorry."

She looked grotesque, her face all crumpled like that. I hated the way she looked. I turned away from her, those nonsense words still tumbling in my head.

You drowned.

Swimming in Maryland.

Two days ago.

No, none of it made sense. Not then, and not later that night when the Earth dipped toward the stars. Not the next morning when it rolled back around to sunlight again.

It didn't make sense that the world could *roll back to sunlight again.*

All this time, I'd thought that our story was just that: our *story. But it turns out you had your own story, and I had mine. Our stories might have overlapped for a while—long enough that they even looked like the same story. But they were different.*

And that made me realize this: Everyone's story is different, all the time. No one is ever really together, even if it looks for a while like they are.

There was a time when my mom knew what had happened to you, when the weight of it had already hit her and I was just running through the grass like it was any other day. And there was a time when someone else knew and my mom didn't. And a time when your mom knew and almost no one else on the planet did.

And that means that there was a time when you were gone and no one on Earth had any idea. Just you, all alone, disappearing into the water and no one even wondering yet.

And that is an incredibly lonely thing to think about.

Sometimes things just happen, *my mom had said. It was a terrible answer, the very worst.*

Mrs. Turton says when something happens that no one can explain, it means you have bumped up against the edge of human knowledge. And that is when you need science. Science is the process for finding the explanations that no one else can give you.

I'll bet you never even met Mrs. Turton.

Sometimes things just happen *is not an explanation. It is not remotely scientific. But for weeks and weeks, that was all I had.*

Until I stood in that basement room looking at jellyfish on the other side of the glass.

invisible

THE JELLIES EXHIBIT, BELOW THE TOUCH TANK, where the rest of my seventh-grade class flicked water at one another, was nearly empty. It was quiet down there, which was a relief.

The room was filled with tanks of jellyfish. I saw jellies whose tentacles were finer than hair; the aquarium must have projected lights into the tank, because the animals kept changing color. Nearby, in a different tank, I looked at jellies whose tentacles swirled the way wisps of a girl's hair might if she floated underwater. In a third tank, the jellies' tentacles were so thick and straight it seemed like the animals had created their own prison. There was even a tank filled with brand-new baby jellies; they looked like tiny, delicate white flowers.

Such strange creatures, all of them—they looked like aliens, almost. Graceful aliens. Silent ones. Like alien ballerinas who danced without needing any music.

Near the corner of the room a sign said AN INVISI-BLE ENIGMA. I knew what *enigma* meant—my mother often said I was one, especially when I dipped fried eggs in grape jelly or deliberately wore mismatched socks. *Enigma* means "mystery." I like mysteries, so I walked over to read the sign. A photograph on the sign showed two fingers holding a tiny jar. Inside the jar, almost impossible to see, floated a transparent jellyfish about the size of a fingernail.

The text explained that the jar held something called an Irukandji jellyfish, whose venom is among the most dangerous in the world. Some even said it was a thousand times as strong as that of a tarantula.

AN IRUKANDJI STING RESULTS IN EXCRU-
CIATING HEADACHE AND BODY PAIN,
VOMITING, SWEATING, ANXIETY, DANGER-
OUSLY FAST HEARTBEAT, BRAIN HEMOR-
RHAGE, AND FLUID IN THE LUNGS. WHEN
STUNG, PATIENTS REPORT A FEELING OF
IMPENDING DOOM; SOME PATIENTS ARE
SO CERTAIN THAT DEATH IS IMMINENT
THEY BEG PHYSICIANS TO KILL THEM SO
THEY CAN "GET IT OVER WITH."

Well. That sounded completely awful. I read on:

INDEED, THERE ARE A NUMBER OF DOCU-
MENTED DEATHS FROM IRUKANDJI SYN-
DROME, AND IT IS UNKNOWN IF IRUKANDJI
STINGS HAVE BEEN THE TRUE CAUSE OF
DEATHS MISTAKENLY ATTRIBUTED TO
OTHER CAUSES. SCIENTISTS ARE TRYING
TO LEARN MORE ABOUT THE VENOM, AND
ABOUT WHETHER THE TRUE IMPACT OF
THE IRUKANDJI STING IS MUCH GREATER
THAN PREVIOUSLY UNDERSTOOD.

WHILE THE IRUKANDJI LIVES IN LARGE
NUMBERS OFF THE COAST OF AUSTRALIA,
IRUKANDJI-LIKE SYMPTOMS HAVE BEEN
EXPERIENCED AS FAR NORTH AS THE
BRITISH ISLES, AND IN HAWAII, FLOR-
IDA, AND JAPAN. AS A RESULT, MANY
RESEARCHERS BELIEVE THE IRUKANDJI
HAS MIGRATED FAR BEYOND ITS NATIVE
AUSTRALIA. AS THE OCEANS WARM, IT IS
LIKELY THAT THE IRUKANDJI, LIKE OTHER
JELLIES, WILL CONTINUE TO MIGRATE OVER
GREATER DISTANCES.

When I finished reading that passage, I read it
again.

Then I read it a third time.

I looked at the photograph, at that transparent
little creature. Nobody would ever see that thing in
the water. It would be completely invisible.

I turned back to the explanation. I stared at those
words for a long time.

Number of documented deaths . . .

Migrate over greater distances . . .

My head buzzed, and I felt a little dizzy. It felt like nothing in the world existed besides me and those words and the silent creatures pulsing all around me.

Mistakenly attributed to other causes . . .

I stared at the words so long that they started looking unfamiliar, like something written in an entirely different language.

It was only when I exhaled that I realized I hadn't been breathing.

My classmates' chattering returned to me then, and I hurried back up the stairs to the touch tank room where I'd left them.

But upstairs, everything was different. The bearded aquarium worker had been replaced by a woman with a blonde ponytail. She said all the same things into the microphone—*hands flat, keep still.* The tie-dye T-shirts of my classmates had also disappeared; the touch tank room was now filled with kids in uniforms of khaki and plaid. This was a different school group altogether.

I wondered if my classmates had gone back to the Eugene Field Memorial Middle School without me.

I stepped out into the main part of the aquarium and looked around. It didn't take long for me to spot those tie-dye T-shirts. They snaked around a giant ocean tank like a school of mottled, neon-colored fish.

They hadn't even bothered to visit the JELLIES exhibit. They knew nothing about the Irukandji. They would never even wonder.

I understood then: Nobody would ever wonder. Nobody but me.

how to make a friend

*T*HE FIRST TIME I SEE YOU, YOU ARE WEAR-*ing a light blue bathing suit. It is the color of a summer sky, with sparkles all over it like stars, and it looks like day and night are happening at the same time.*

I am five years old, and I am starting kindergarten soon. We are at the big pool that is indoors. It is loud here. Everything echoes. The moms are sitting behind us on bleachers. They've brought us here, to this class they call Guppies, so we can learn to put our faces in the water and kick.

The teacher blows a whistle, calling kids' names one at a time. We are supposed to hold on to a foam board and kick and let her pull us around the shallow end. But you don't jump in when she calls your name, and I don't jump in when she calls mine, either.

Your hair looks like straw in sunlight. I like your freckles, the way they look like constellations against your skin.

When we are the last ones sitting there, just the two of us at the edge of the pool, the teacher with the whistle comes over to us. She says, Sorry, girls, it's time to join the class.

I am about to shake my head no when you turn to me. You look right at me, and I see your pink lips part. A smile. Then you take a deep breath and lower yourself into the water. The teacher hands you a foam board, but you don't take it.

Instead, you go underwater. Your eyes, hair, everything. And you swim. All the way over to where the rest of the kids are clinging to their boards. Underwater the whole way.

I follow you. I lower myself into the water, not because the lady tells me to but because I want to swim like you can. And because I like your freckles and your sunstraw hair and the smile you showed me. And because at this moment, making a friend, and having one, seems like the easiest thing in the world.

150 million stings

WHEN I ARRIVED HOME ON THE AFTER-
noon of the aquarium trip, I was surprised
to see my brother's Jeep nosed up right next to my
mom's car. Next to Aaron's Jeep, cross-legged on the
driveway, sat his boyfriend, Rocco.

I'd spent most of the bus ride home thinking about
jellyfish. A sign next to one of the tanks had said that
there are 150 million jellyfish stings every year. So during the ride back to school—while the other kids yelled
and played music and threw notes from seat to seat and
tried to get truck drivers to honk their horns—I'd made
some calculations in the back of my science notebook.

One hundred fifty million stings a year is equal to almost 411,000 stings every day, which is equal to 17,000 jellyfish stings every hour.

And that means four to five stings every single second.

I'd closed my eyes and counted to five. By the time I was finished, something like twenty-three people had just been stung.

Then I did it again. *One, two, three, four, five.* Another twenty-three people.

I counted again and again. I counted so much that the counting and the stings started to seem like the same thing—as if instead of measuring the stings, I was somehow causing them. And even though I knew that couldn't be true, some part of me almost believed it: like, if only I could just stop counting, maybe I could make the stings stop.

But I couldn't stop counting to five. It was like one part of my brain insisted on defying another part of my brain.

Rocco squinted up at me from the asphalt. "Well, hey there, Suzy Q ," he said. "Beautiful day, huh?"

I didn't answer him. He must have known I wouldn't.

He waved his hand toward the sky. *"If I were a bird,"* he said, *"I would fly about the earth seeking the successive autumns. . . ."*

He barely seemed to be talking to me. I liked that. It was like watching someone's private thoughts, as if I were both there and not-there at the same time.

"George Eliot," he added, and I nodded, as if I knew who that was. Rocco is a graduate student in English literature at the university where Aaron coaches women's soccer. Rocco is always quoting someone.

If I were the type of person who still said things, I might have said to Rocco: *Count to five.* And when he was done counting, I could have told him about the twenty-three stings.

Then I'd have made him do it again. And I'd have said: *Forty-six stings.*

And again. *Sixty-nine.*

Rocco interrupted my thoughts. "Aaron and I stopped by to see if we could convince you and your mom to go to the movies," he said. "But she says you have a doctor's appointment or something."

The doctor I could talk to. Ugh.

Then he grinned. "Your mom, of course, took this as an opportunity to pass on some of her 'treasures.' She's loading Aaron up now."

He emphasized that word—*treasures*—and I had to smile. Mom likes shopping at thrift stores—she calls it treasure hunting, though I have never figured out what exactly makes somebody's discarded fondue set or chipped flowerpot a *treasure*. Mom just can't resist what she thinks is a bargain. Our house is filled with boxes of oddball items like jars filled with buttons (she doesn't sew), and muffin tins (she doesn't bake), and knitting needles held together with masking tape (she doesn't knit).

Rocco patted the asphalt next to him. "Sit." It was nice to be asked, but I needed to keep thinking about those stings. I shook my head, then gave a tiny wave goodbye. Rocco saluted me, closed his eyes, and lifted his face toward the sun.

I walked toward the house, adding numbers as fast as I could.

One hundred and fifteen stings.

One hundred and thirty-eight.

One hundred and sixty-one.

Inside the house, Aaron stood near the front door, holding a cardboard box overflowing with kitchen-ware: a yellow metal platter covered with roosters, an eggbeater, a worn-out-looking waffle maker with the price tag ($3.97) still visible.

"Well, well, well. Look who's here." Aaron grinned at me. My brother. Tanned and athletic, always ready with an easy smile. Sometimes Aaron seemed almost too good to be true.

Mom poked her head out of the kitchen. "Zu," she said, and she winked at me. She has called me that forever. Zu is her nickname for *Suzy*, which is funny, because *Suzy* is already a nickname for *Suzanne*. Once, a few years ago, I tried to get her to call me simply Z, the shortest nickname of all, but it never took. "We're leaving for your appointment in fifteen minutes. Your dad's meeting us there."

Mom wore her work clothes, the pantsuit she wears whenever she shows houses. Her shoes were off, though, and her frizzy hair—I inherited my wild mop from her—had fallen out of its bun.

She placed some salad tongs on top of Aaron's box.

"Ma," Aaron said. "We don't need any more stuff."

"Hold on a sec," she said. "I've got a cutting board I want to give you." She squatted down on the kitchen floor, opened up a cabinet, and began rummaging.

"Rocco's waiting, Mom," Aaron said. He looked at me and rolled his eyes. I spun my finger next to my ear as if to say, *Crazy*.

"Hey," he said, just to me now, as Mom rattled pots and pans in the kitchen. "School okay?"

I shrugged.

He looked at me closely. "Suzy, middle school sucks," he said. "You know that, right?"

I looked down at the floor.

"No, really, Suzy. When I was in seventh grade, all I wanted was to get the heck out of there. And

I hadn't even lost my best fr—" He stopped quickly and shook his head. "I'm just saying. It won't always be this way."

When I didn't say anything, he added, "I promise, Suzy."

And just like that, I felt a lump welling up in my throat.

Mom breezed out of the kitchen holding up a cracked wooden board, cut in the shape of a pig. "Found it! You must need a cutting board. Everyone needs a decent cutting board."

She placed it on top of the box and Aaron laughed. "Hmmm," he said, frowning at the pig-shaped slab. "Maybe not *that* cutting board, though..."

Mom slapped him gently on the arm. "You be nice to your ol' mom."

"Okay, but can my ol' mom let me get to the movies?"

"Yes, of course," she said with a sigh. "I'll set aside a pile of kitchen stuff and save it for you later."

I walked to my room as my brother called down the hallway, "See ya next time, Suzy!"

I sat down at my desk and opened my notebook. I started a new count.

One...two...three...four...

Through the window, I watched Aaron walk toward Rocco.

Twenty-three stings.

Jellyfish were stinging every single second of every single minute of every single day.

Rocco stood, took the box from Aaron's hands, and carried it over to the car.

Forty-six stings.

They were stinging day after day, week after week, month after month, year after year.

Rocco set the box down in the backseat.

Sixty-nine stings.

He picked up the pig cutting board and looked at Aaron. Aaron shrugged, as if saying to Rocco, *That's my mom for ya.*

Ninety-two.

Then they got in the car and shut the doors. Through the windshield, I saw Rocco rumple Aaron's hair. They looked like they were laughing.

They leaned toward each other and kissed before Aaron backed the car out of the driveway. Then they were off—headed to the movies, to the kind of life people get to have when their words don't ruin everything.

Seeing them, all that easy happiness, made me feel mixed up inside. It was like I could remember happiness, but also couldn't remember it, all at the same time.

Mostly, though, I knew I didn't deserve happiness. Would never deserve it ever again.

part two

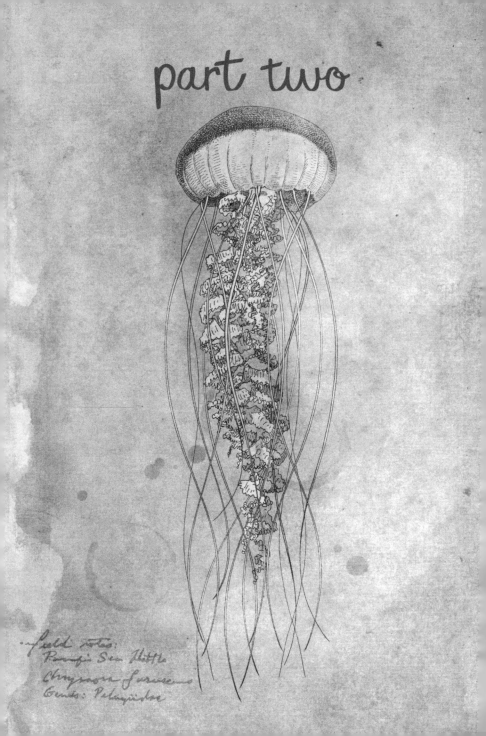

field notes:
Pacific Sea Nettle
Chrysaora fuscescens
Genus: Pelagiidae

Hypothesis

A hypothesis is a tentative explanation, a proposed answer to the question that underlies your research. Think of it as your best educated guess.

—MRS. TURTON

best educated guess

AFTER AARON AND ROCCO LEFT, I OPENED my notebook and began writing:

- There are 7 billion people on the planet.
- There are 150 million jellyfish stings every year.
- Seven billion divided by 150 million is 46.6.
- That means there is one jellyfish sting for every 46.6 people.
- There is no such thing as .6 of a person, of course—so what I really

mean is one jellyfish sting for every
46 or 47 people.

- I know many more people than that
in real life.
- There is a good probability, then, that
I know at least one person who has
been stung by a jellyfish.
- No one has ever told me that they have
been stung by a jellyfish.
- It is likely, then, that the person I
know who has been stung by a jellyfish
didn't tell me.
- Maybe she didn't tell me because she
couldn't.
- Maybe she couldn't tell me because she
is dead.
- Maybe she is dead because of that
jellyfish sting.

I put down my pen and sat quietly for a long moment.
From downstairs, I heard my mother calling my name,
but I was too busy thinking to answer.

Maybe Mom was wrong. Maybe things don't *just*

happen, like she'd tried to tell me. Maybe things aren't actually as random as everyone seemed ready to accept.

Things had ended between me and Franny in the worst way. If I'd known, I'd have said sorry for the way things happened. I'd have at least said goodbye. But a person doesn't always know the difference between a new beginning and a forever sort of ending. Now it was too late to fix any of it.

But maybe I could still do something. Maybe I could prove that there was an actual villain in Franny's story. A villain worse than me.

I picked up my pen again, and I wrote:

HYPOTHESIS: That the Worst Thing was caused by a sting from an Irukandji jellyfish.

That's when my door burst open. Mom stood in the doorway with a very angry look on her face.

"Zu," she said. Her voice was sharp. "Come *on*."

I closed my notebook. And just like that, we were off to *the doctor I could talk to*, even though anyone who knew me should have known that I wasn't going to say anything at all.

part three

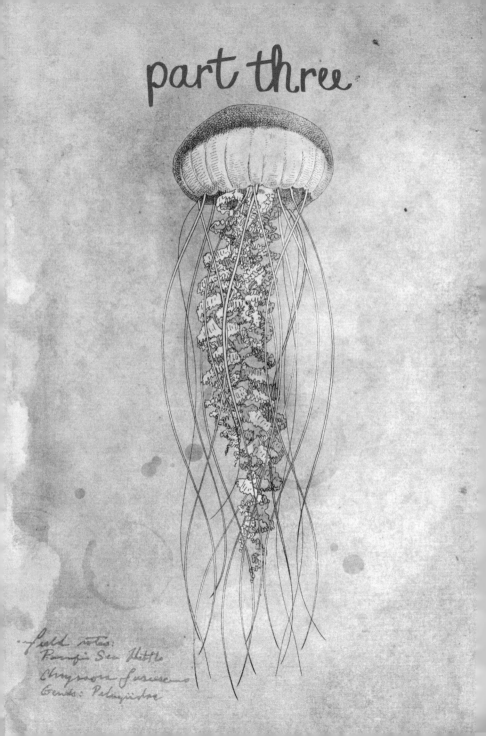

field notes:
Pacific Sea Nettle
Chrysaora fuscescens
Genus: Pelagiidae

Background

Your background provides the context for your
scientific quest. What do we already know? What
don't we know? Why does it matter?

—MRS. TURTON

early life

I COULD TELL YOU A LOT ABOUT JELLYFISH. THE first thing I want to tell you is this: They are older than dinosaurs, older than insects, older than trees or flowers or ferns or fungi or seeds. They are at least 600 million years old, probably older than any type of living thing you've ever seen with your eyes or imagined inside your brain.

There have been five mass extinctions since jellyfish showed up on the scene. One of those extinctions, the Great Dying, killed off nine out of ten species on Earth. Picture that. It would be like going to the zoo and discovering that nearly all the animals had vanished. Maybe all the cages are empty except for a handful of birds, a small rodent or two, a couple of clams and snails. Everything else is just gone, *poof,* their cages forever barren.

It's not just mass extinctions that wipe out species, either. Almost every species that has ever existed has already disappeared forever.

But here's the thing: All that dying, all those extinctions? They didn't do a thing to jellyfish.

If you could build a bridge from where we are today—a time of peacocks and giraffes, monarch butterflies and human beings who shove each other into lockers—back to the beginning of what most of us think of as life itself, that bridge would be jellyfish.

Jellyfish separate the world that *was* from the one that *is.*

Here's a calculation: If all the time that's passed since jellyfish showed up were compressed into a single eighty-year life-span, three billion heartbeats, humans would appear on the scene only during the person's final ten days on Earth—the last million heartbeats or so. Jellyfish would have been around for everything else—birth, infancy, toddlerhood, childhood. We humans would appear only to witness those final, gasping breaths.

And if it is true what they say, if it is true that the sixth mass extinction is going on right this minute, if the world around us is dying in ways we cannot even imagine, then maybe this is the end of us, too, and of everything we know.

And that is a very scary thing to think about.

But the main thing to know is this: The whole time, from before any of those extinctions, from life's origins until this minute, jellyfish have been there, pulsing their way across the oceans and back.

Jellyfish are survivors. They are survivors of everything that ever happened to everyone else.

how to have a friend

*W*E ARE OUTSIDE, AND IT IS SUMMER. YOUR mother is letting us stay up later than we usually do—later, she says, than seven-year-olds should. You and I started the evening at my house. We planned a sleepover there—it would be the first time you slept away from your own home. But after dinner you changed your mind and cried, and so my mom called your mom, and then your mom picked us up.

Now we are sleeping at your house instead.

We are running and running in circles. The sky above us grows dim, and dark figures swoop around in the air above us. I am pretty sure they are bats. I tell you this, and you squeal. We run faster.

I know some things about bats. I know that bats are the only mammal that can fly, because that is something I read in a book.

I am a good reader now, and sometimes I tell you about the things I read, and you ask me to tell you even more. Like when I told you that rabbits' teeth never stop growing, you wanted me to tell you everything else I knew about rabbits—that they cannot throw up and that they will eat their own poop and that the longest rabbit ears ever seen were thirty-one inches.

*My parents have a word for what I do—*constant-talking, *like that is a single word—and they explain to me that it is important to let others talk, too.* Ask people questions, *my mom always says.* It's not a conversation if you're constant-talking. *And I try to remember that, to ask people things.*

But you like it when I tell you things. You don't need me to ask you questions. You have never once called what I do constant-talking.

We spread our arms like wings, and when we fall down in the grass, we breathe hard and laugh and the world moves around us in dizzy ways.

Fluffernutter, your dog, watches. She is still just a

puppy, a little ball of white fur. As we run, she yips and wags her tail, which is really just a stump because someone cut it off when she was born. Fluffernutter is tied to a leash, which is looped over a stick in the ground; it would take nothing at all for Fluffernutter to pull the stick out and come running after us, but she doesn't. She thinks she is more trapped than she actually is.

And you know what? I don't care that we are not at my house like we planned, and I don't care that you still use a sippy cup at night, even though we are almost in second grade. I don't care that you sometimes cry because you miss your daddy, who you don't even remember. I don't care that you write your Ns backward and that you sometimes read nap instead of pan, which means you have to go to summer school this year. I don't care that your cheeks and your neck and your ears flush bright pink when you are asked to read out loud in class, or that you sometimes have trouble coming up with ideas for a story. I have plenty of ideas for both of us.

I also don't care that at the end of the school year, a girl named Aubrey said, loudly enough that everyone could hear, "Franny Jackson isn't pretty or smart."

I saw your face when she said that. I saw the way your cheeks got blotchy, saw the way you stared at the ground as if you could hold the tears in. But you couldn't, and you started crying, and you cried for almost all of recess, until I whispered to you that the playground was really ancient Egypt and that the space between the swing set and the slide was the Nile River. If we ran through that space fast enough, maybe we could avoid the crocodiles. And that made you smile even though you still had some snot in your nose, and it didn't take long before we were both running and laughing like usual.

So I don't care about those other girls, just like I don't care that in my end-of-first-grade report card the teacher said perhaps you and I should try to make some other friends, that perhaps "branching out" would help me with my "social skills," whatever those things mean.

The teacher doesn't understand. She doesn't understand that we have everything we need, exactly as we are. Like right now: We have the grass under our feet and Fluffernutter's wagging stump and the spinning and the laughter and the sky growing dark above our heads.

dr. legs

MOM AND I SAT IN THE CAR, IN THE PARK-
ing lot of the First Street Schoolhouse
building. Which, for the record, is actually on Garis
Street, and it isn't a school at all. It's a bunch of
offices, one of which happens to belong to Dr. M.
Legler, child psychologist.

Through the windshield, I saw my dad waiting for
us to get out of the car.

"Zu," my mom said. "Please don't make us any
later than we already are."

I folded my arms across my chest. Otherwise, I
stayed exactly still.

"Listen, Zu. The fact that we're here doesn't mean we think something's wrong with you."

You think I'm cray cray. That's why we're here.

As if she could hear my thoughts, Mom added, "I know you're sad, Zu, but I'm also sure you're going to be okay. But your dad and I—"

She sighed and looked out at him. Held up her index finger, as if to say, *Just a moment.* He nodded and waved.

"We want to make sure we're doing everything we can to help you." She sighed again. "Other than giving you time, this is the only thing we could think to do."

When I didn't say anything, she added, "I know you don't want to be here, Zu. But I'm going to ask you to get out of the car anyway."

I frowned. But I opened the car door.

"Hey, kiddo," Dad greeted me. "How are you?" His voice was all friendly, as if we weren't in that parking lot because of my cracks and flaws. As if he didn't call my mom to talk about my *not-talking* all the time. Mom always pretended she was getting a work call, but I could hear her saying things like *I don't know, Jim.... No, I have no earthly idea why.... I swear.... Yes, I'm trying. Of* course *I have told her that.*

My dad wrapped his arm around me and pulled me toward him in a half-hug, as if I might just answer, *Great, Dad, I'm doing great.*

We walked through the door and up to suite 307, which is the one with Dr. M. Legler's name on it.

The doctor I could talk to was different than I expected. For one thing, Dr. M. Legler was a woman. For another, she had jet-black hair, straight, like a vampire's. Her legs stretched long and thin beneath a short skirt, and she wore lacy black tights, which I frankly didn't think was very professional.

Dr. Legs, I thought. I frowned.

She led us into an office with a thick carpet and leather chairs and gestured for us to sit.

The chair squeaked as I settled into it.

Dr. Legs looked directly at me. "Your parents called me, Suzanne, because they're worried about you."

I looked away, toward the window, even though all I could see was a different window, shade drawn, surrounded by a brick wall.

"They tell me you're pretty quiet these days. Is that right?"

I folded my arms, my eyes still on that window. If she knew that, why in the world would she think I would answer her question? For that matter, why was she asking a question she clearly already had the answer to?

"And they say you stopped talking soon after the loss of your friend, is that right?"

Not my friend, I thought. *Not when it happened, anyway.*

"Well, I want you to know," she continued, as if I'd answered her, "everybody grieves in different ways. There's not a right way or a wrong way to grieve for someone you loved."

I looked at her bookshelf. It was filled with books that had titles like *The Miracle of Mindfulness. Victims No Longer. Overcoming Depression One Step at a Time. No More Bedwetting.*

As Dr. Legs spoke, I imagined rearranging the words in the titles.

No More Time.

One-Step Depression.

Victims of the Bedwetting Miracle.

"Meg." Dr. Legs turned to my mom. "How does Suzanne's refusal to talk affect you?"

Sometimes my mother's tears are sad tears, sometimes they're happy tears, and sometimes they're what she calls love tears, but I can't always tell the difference between them. I watched her eyes fill, and I thought: *These are probably the sad kind.*

"Suzy just seems so…unhappy," my mom said. Her voice was quieter and heavier than I wanted it to be.

It seemed mean to ask my mom to talk about something that made her cry. Frankly, I didn't much care for Dr. Legs's character.

When my mom was done explaining how she just really wanted to be let in, Dr. Legs turned to my dad.

"Tell me, Jim," she said. "How often do you see Suzanne?"

"Every week," he said. "Every Saturday night."

"And you stick to that routine?"

"Always."

It was true. Every Saturday, without fail, Dad and I went to Ming Palace, a Chinese restaurant wedged between Planet Fitness and the Price Chopper supermarket out on Route 24. It was a promise Dad had made when he moved out: that no matter how much he had to travel the rest of the week, he would be there on Saturday at 6 p.m. Every single week.

"Do you see the same thing as Meg?" Dr. Legs asked. "Do you think Suzanne is unhappy?"

"What do *you* think?" he snapped. He frowned and took a deep breath. "I'm sorry. But I mean...of course she's unhappy. That's why we're here."

He looked at the floor. When he spoke again, his voice was quiet. "Maybe I could deal with the silence better if we still lived together," he said. "But I'm not at the house to tell her good night. And I'm not there when she's getting ready for school in the morning. And I'm not there when she does her homework.

I travel all the time, and I spend all week looking forward to weekends. But now—now she doesn't even talk to me, and it's like I've got nothing at all. Like she's just...gone."

Sometimes, when I don't like what is happening, I make lists of things in my head. I decided right then to make a list of the most interesting things I could remember seeing online.

I once saw pictures of two blonde girls, laughing and making faces at each other, and it all looked very friendly and usual, except that their two necks stemmed out of a single body.

I once saw a man with devil horns surgically implanted in his head and tattoos all over his face. I didn't especially enjoy seeing that.

I once saw a polar bear that had starved to death. The bear had needed ice to find food, but all the ice had melted. The bear was skin and bones, like a lumpy white rug, lying on green grass with one paw lifted up in a kind of salute.

I hated seeing that.

"Suzanne," Dr. Legs was saying. "I'm going to ask

you to try to trust me. You can say anything here. Anything at all. I won't judge."

I nodded, because it seemed like that was what the situation called for. But by then I had stopped listening. All I really wanted to do was get back to a computer and start looking up everything I could about jellyfish. I wasn't sure how a person even begins to go about testing a hypothesis like the one I'd formed, and I knew I didn't have any time to waste.

Dr. Legs finished whatever she was saying with the words "... and that's why we sometimes need the help of a *professional*."

I looked up. I wasn't sure what exactly she had been saying, but that word, *professional*, seemed important.

"You see, *professionals* are trained to recognize patterns," she continued. "Both good patterns and the patterns that a person might want to change. Professionals are trained to help people figure out things they struggle to understand on their own."

Right then, an idea dawned on me.

"I mean," Dr. Legs continued, "a twelve-year-old can't be expected to solve *every* problem herself, can she?"

She was absolutely right. I did need a professional. Not for the *not-talking*, of course. But to help me with my hypothesis.

There had to be jellyfish experts out there—people who knew about migration patterns, or stings, or other things I wouldn't even think to wonder about on my own.

Jellyologists, I thought. *I need a jellyologist.*

I was going to find some. And one of them was going to help me prove the thing I needed to prove: that Franny had been stung by a jellyfish.

If any part of me questioned this mission right then, if any part of me thought, *This is a crazy notion—it is filled with cracks and flaws*, I pushed it out of my brain immediately.

The thing is, a person gets so few chances to really fix something, to make it right. When one of those opportunities comes along, you can't overthink it. You've got to grab hold of it and cling to it with all your might, no matter how *cray cray* it might seem.

Outside, in the parking lot, Dad gave me a hug. "See you on Saturday," he said. He had picked up a brochure in the office: *Children and Grief: Big Issues for Little Hearts*. "Same time, same place."

Then he kissed me on the top of my head. He got into his car, and my mom and I got into her car, and everybody drove away from the First Street Schoolhouse building.

For now.

dumb old words

MING PALACE WAS THE PLACE WHERE MY not-talking began. It was just a few days after seventh grade started, which was just a few days after Franny's funeral. When I arrived at the restaurant that night, Dad was outside, cradling a phone between his neck and his shoulder. "Uh-huh," he said. He held up one finger as if to say, *I'll be just a moment*.

Dad's job is something confusing with computers and universities. His travel involves something called *systems checks*, which sounds kind of tedious to me.

"Yeah, that's what I was saying," he said into the

phone. "Yup. Seems to be isolated to that server.... Yeah, they've got all their resources on it."

He smiled at me and rolled his eyes, as if to say, *These guys*, about whoever he was talking to.

I smiled back and rolled my own eyes, as if to say, *Yeah, I know just what you mean.*

I had no idea who he was talking to.

When he finally hung up, he put his arm around my shoulder and pulled me in for a quick hug. "Sorry about that, kiddo. Crisis resolved for the moment."

I followed him into the restaurant, and we sat down in the pink vinyl booth we always chose. The waitress came over. "You want the usual?" she asked. After more than a year of Saturday dinners out, she knows our order by heart: wonton soup (me), hot and sour (Dad), honey chicken with rice (me), moo shu pork (Dad), Shirley Temple (me), Rolling Rock (Dad).

I nodded, and Dad nodded. Then he turned to me. "So what did you think about your first couple of days of school?"

By now I was twelve years old and starting my second year of middle school. I knew a few things about grown-ups. And here's one of the things I knew: Grown-ups are like everybody else—they don't actually want you to say what you're thinking.

Once, when my dad asked me what I was thinking, I told him about the Great Pacific Garbage Vortex, which is like a stew of plastic trash that gets swirled together smack-dab in the middle of the Pacific Ocean. I told him that some people think the Garbage Vortex is two times the size of the state of Texas, and that it's filled with plastic that people dump in the ocean, and that the plastic chokes the coral and gets rocked by the waves, and then breaks down into tiny pieces. Then grown-up birds confuse those plastic scraps with food and feed them to their chicks, and the babies die of starvation even though their parents are feeding them just like they should.

My dad had sighed when I told him that. I guess he wanted me to tell him about gym class instead.

My dad's question hung in the air. What did I think about my first couple of days of school?

What my dad wanted, I suspect, was the thing

everybody seems to want: small talk. But I don't understand small talk. I don't even understand why it's called that—small talk—when it fills up so much space.

Most of all, I don't understand why small talk is considered more polite than *not-talking*. It's like when people applaud after a performance. Have you ever heard someone *not* clap after a performance? People clap every time, no matter whether it was good or bad. They even applaud after the Eugene Field band plays its annual concert, and that's *really* saying something. So wouldn't it be easier and take less time and effort to just *not clap*? Because it would mean the same thing, which is nothing at all.

In the end, *not-talking* means the same thing, more or less, as small talk. Nothing. Besides, I'll bet so-called small talk has ended more friendships than silence ever did.

After a while, my dad tried again. "Anyone you especially like? Teachers? New kids?"

I thought about that. For the most part, it was a lot of the same kids I knew from previous years:

wretched Dylan Parker and messy-always-messing-up Justin Maloney. That new girl, Sarah Johnston, seemed okay, I guess. And I was pretty sure I liked Mrs. Turton, the seventh-grade science teacher. When we walked in the door on the first day, she wore an Albert Einstein wig and tried to explain that time moves at different speeds depending on how fast you're traveling. I liked the way she made it seem like the world around us, even the normal everyday stuff, was actually kind of amazing. Already, she'd told us there are 60,000 miles of blood vessels in a single human body, enough to circle Earth two and a half times. She told us that ants sleep for just eight minutes a day but that snails can sleep for three years. She also said that each of us has at least 20 billion atoms from William Shakespeare inside our body. *At least* 20 billion, she emphasized, and she showed us some complicated math to prove it.

I tried feeling those atoms, tried to sense if there was anything inside me that might inspire me to burst out with *To be, or not to be* or *Wherefore art thou*, but I couldn't. Then I realized that if we all had Shakespeare's atoms inside us, we probably also had atoms from Adolf Hitler, who was probably the worst human who ever lived. And I didn't really want to think about that.

I liked that we were going to write research papers for Mrs. Turton's class and that we could choose any subject we wanted as long as it related to science. Past students, she explained, had studied orcas, diabetes, astronaut food, the Black Death, velociraptors, solar hurricanes, and bioterrorism. The point, she said, was to learn how to research, how to find out more about anything we wondered about. "That's what science is," she explained. "It's learning what others have discovered about the world, and then— when you bump up against a question that no one has ever answered before—figuring out how to get the answer you need."

So I could have told my dad about those things, but I didn't. Instead, I listened to the sounds around me—the rumble of ice from the drink machine, the ding of a cash register, the murmur of voices, and the occasional burst of laughter from nearby tables.

I liked these sounds. They were better than any dumb old words.

Dumb old words that don't mean a thing.

Dumb old words that fill up too much space.

Dumb old words that sometimes end friendships forever.

"What, aren't you speaking to me tonight?" Dad laughed, like it was a joke.

That's when I thought, *What if I never made small talk again?* It seemed like a good idea: Either say something important, or say nothing.

Dad made a grumpy face. "Okay, Suzy," he said. He sounded exasperated. "You just let me know when you're ready to make conversation."

But I had already decided: I wasn't going to make conversation. Not that night, and maybe not ever again.

And in the four weeks that had passed since then, I hadn't.

expert #1

THE NIGHT WE GOT HOME FROM SEEING Dr. Legs, I began my research. I found a bunch of jellyfish experts, actually. I found a guy in Rhode Island who studies how jellyfish move through the water. A grandmotherly lady who studies jellyfish populations near Seattle. A guy in Washington, DC, who studies how they evolved. I clicked on researcher after researcher, ruling out one after another—one just because he didn't list an e-mail or any contact information, another because she wrote articles filled with words I didn't understand, words like *pharmacognosy*, *methanolic*, and *eosin*. The grandmotherly researcher looked like an older version of my mother, and I didn't want to imagine my mother growing old.

Then I found someone I thought might be interesting.

I pulled out my notebook and began to write:

POSSIBLE EXPERT #1:
<u>Dhugal Lindsay, Japan</u>
Glasses and brown hair. Works at a lab where scientists send remote-control vehicles into the deep sea. He discovered a never-before-seen jellyfish in the darkest part of the ocean. It had a red part inside the bell that could crumple or expand, just like a folding paper lantern. Named it the Paper Lantern jellyfish. I like how literal that is.

Writes haiku poetry about things he sees. Here is one:

soap bubbles
westward to nirvana each
carrying nothing

Well. That is not nearly literal enough.

Advantages:

- Face looks nice. Soft eyes. Not-mean.
- Discovers new things, which means he knows there is more in the world than what has already been discovered.

Disadvantages:

- Very far away.
- Does not seem to write about Irukandji or any sort of venom.
- Might ask me to read his poetry.

Conclusion:

- Rejected for reasons related to poetry.

mote of dust

BEFORE EVERY SCIENCE CLASS, MRS. TURTON always spent a few minutes telling us some-thing about the world that she thought we might find interesting. We might get ideas for our science reports, she said.

Or, she added with a grin, we might just get ideas.

On the day after our aquarium visit, we walked into Mrs. Turton's classroom and saw a quote on the blackboard: *a mote of dust suspended in a sunbeam.*

"Settle down, settle down," Mrs. Turton said as we took our seats. "First of all, if you have not yet picked a topic for your science report, *please, please* come and talk to me after class. You should be well into researching it by now."

She placed her hands on a desk in the front row and said, "Let me repeat myself." She looked right at me, and I knew then that I was probably the last person in the class to pick a topic. "It's time to begin your research."

I stared right back at her without blinking. I finally knew what my research project would be.

"Are there any questions?" she asked.

Nobody raised their hands.

"Okay, so before we begin, I want to take a few minutes and journey back in time," she said. "Christmas 1968. Most of your parents haven't even been born. There's no Internet, no e-mail, no texting or video games or cell phones. But there are spaceships, which are so brand-new that they seem like the stuff of science fiction."

She paused. The whole class sat still.

"A few days before Christmas, the spacecraft *Apollo 8* leaves the planet. Then, on Christmas Eve, the astronauts send *this* image back to Earth from outer space."

She clicked a button on her remote control, and a photograph appeared on the screen at the front of the room. I'd seen the picture before: Earth rising above the surface of the moon. The planet looked like a giant swirling blue marble, half a marble, really, surrounded by blackness.

"I know you guys have grown up with this image," she said. "But I want you to try to imagine what it must have been like to see it for the first time. To be the first humans alive, ever, to see our Earth, in full color, from the outside."

I stared at the image on the screen. Earth looked alive, vibrant. The moon was desolate and gray by comparison. Mrs. Turton clicked the remote control again, and the image disappeared. In its place was another photograph of outer space. This picture was mostly dark, with just a few pale brownish rays of light streaking across.

"Now," she said. "Here's a different view."

She pointed to the middle of one of those rays, at a tiny, faint dot. A bunch of kids had to squint and lean closer just to see it.

"That, right there, is us," she said. "That's Earth."

Justin Maloney leaned so far forward that he knocked his books and folders off his desk. Lined notebook paper sprayed across the floor.

"This photo," Mrs. Turton explained, "was taken more recently, from about three billion miles away."

Her finger still on the dot, she said, "That, my friends, is your home. That is where you live, your place inside this solar system. Your whole life—the lives of everyone you will ever see—will likely unfold on this one speck, which a famous cosmologist named Carl Sagan once called 'a mote of dust suspended in a sunbeam.'"

I thought about what Mrs. Turton was saying. Here I was, just one out of seven billion people, and people were just one species out of ten million, and those ten million were just a tiny fraction of all the species that ever existed, and somehow all of us fit onto that fleck of brown dust on the screen. And we were surrounded by nothingness. Just a whole lot of lifeless, lonely nothing in every direction.

And that's when I got a little panicky, a little sick to my stomach.

I liked the view from 1968 so much better. In the 1968 view, we mattered. I wished we hadn't gone any farther out, that we hadn't tried to see ourselves from the outer edge of the solar system. I wished we hadn't seen ourselves as a speck of dust, surrounded by so much nothing we were barely even visible.

"Food for thought," Mrs. Turton said. She flicked off the screen. "And now to our lesson. Today, my darling seventh graders, will be your first day working in the laboratory. The lab is a bit like space, in a way. It is where humans become explorers. It is where scientists push the boundaries of knowledge. And to start you on your journey, we will be studying pond water from our own valley."

I knew about labs, knew we would be studying cells and life systems this year, and that by midyear, we would dissect an earthworm.

"Your first task," Mrs. Turton said, "is to pick your lab partner. Pick wisely, because you'll be together all year. Groups of two, please."

Dylan grabbed a boy named Kevin O'Connor, who also has a reputation for being good-looking but not very nice. For a moment, it looked like the new girl, Sarah Johnston, was coming toward me. She even looked right at me, and I swear she might have smiled, so I got a tiny bit hopeful. Then Aubrey grabbed her and linked her own elbow in Sarah's. I stood there feeling stupid as my classmates paired off, until only one other person was standing alone.

And that person was Justin Maloney.

I sighed. If Justin is good at anything, it is messing up. Once, he took a bunch of squares of butter, lifted his shirt, and rubbed the butter all over his belly. Then he ran down the hallway and took a flying leap and landed in a belly flop on the floor. He'd been hoping to slide down the hallway, but instead he rubbed a bunch of skin off his stomach and spent the rest of the day holding the shirt away from him so his belly wouldn't burn.

As Mrs. Turton explained the lab—observe pond water and tap water, and test pH of each—Justin and I looked at each other. He wore a stopwatch around his neck, and his hair was buzzed almost all the way down to his head.

"Hey, Suzy," Justin said. "I guess we're partners?"

When I didn't respond, he looked down. "Well," he said. "I guess I'll go get the pond water. If that's okay."

I shrugged.

When Justin scooped the water into a jar, drops splashed everywhere. I filled up another jar with tap water; then together we walked to the back corner of the room.

When we sat down, the stopwatch around Justin's neck started beeping. He pushed the stop button, reached into the pocket of his jeans, and pulled out a pale orange tablet. He blew some pocket lint off it, placed it on his tongue, and then swallowed without any water or anything.

Then he looked at me and shrugged. "Breakfast of champions. Or lunch of champions. Whatever."

When I didn't say anything, he explained. "ADHD," he said. "If I don't take it, my brain goes all wacko."

I wasn't sure he should be taking medicine in class, but Justin has never exactly been a rule follower.

I shrugged and returned to work. After a few minutes of dipping pH strips in water and noting our observations on paper, Justin looked up.

"Listen, Suzy," he said. "I know I'm probably not your top pick for a lab partner."

Probably?

"But I won't mess it up for you, okay?"

I searched his face for any kind of sarcasm, but he looked genuine. "With this new medicine I'm on, I'm doing a lot better. I'll work hard, I promise."

When I didn't respond, he returned to writing, mouthing the words as he wrote.

Walking out of class that day, Mrs. Turton stopped me. "Suzanne?"

I stopped.

"Do you have a report topic?"

I nodded.

"You do?" She sounded surprised.

I nodded again, this time looking right at her.

"That's great, Suzanne. What is it?"

Even when you are a not-talker, there are times in life when you have to say something out loud. This was one of those times. In instances like these, it's best to say as little as possible—even just a single word if you can get away with it.

"Jellyfish," I mumbled.

She leaned in like she couldn't hear me. "I'm sorry?"

I frowned and said it louder. "Jellyfish." I knew I sounded annoyed, and I felt bad about that. But once you've committed to not-talking, it can be hard to say anything out loud, let alone repeat yourself.

I guess my tone didn't bother her, though, because she brightened. "That's a terrific topic. There are so many things to learn about any one species—the animal's habitat and range, eating and hunting behavior, its relationship to humans. You let me know if you need any help finding information."

I nodded and started to walk toward the door.

"Suzanne?" She stopped me.

I looked at her.

"You do know that the report is an oral report, right?"

I waited.

"What I mean to say is that you'll have to present your report in front of the class. You can *read* it if you want—it doesn't have to be off the top of your head. And I'll help you practice if you need that. But public speaking is an important part of the grade." She looked at me intently. "Do you understand?"

I nodded. If I wanted to pass seventh-grade science, I was going to have to speak out loud.

how to make
a promise

WE ARE SUPPOSED TO BE LEARNING ABOUT explorers. Instead, we're holding hairbrushes and dancing around your room.

Now that we're in fourth grade, we have tests, and for our next test we have to memorize fifteen different people who helped map the world. You had trouble remembering them, so I started thinking of tricks that could help.

We remembered that Magellan circumnavigated the world by thinking of him as Ma-Jell-O; his body just wiggled and jiggled all over the globe. We remembered Hernando de Soto, who was the first European to explore what is now the southern United States, as Hernando de Soda: It was so hot down south that he needed a soda. We remembered Erik the Red, the Viking who founded the first European settlement on Greenland, as being color-blind; he wanted to name the landmass after himself, but he got confused and named it Green. To remember Captain James Cook, who sailed to Australia, we just needed to remember him as the cook in a restaurant that catered exclusively to koalas and kangaroos.

We decided to take a break after that one. Now we are jumping around and singing like rock stars onstage. We take turns dancing on the bed, then leaping off.

I wave like a princess, my nose high in the air.

"You look like Aubrey," you tell me, and I make a face.

Yesterday on the playground, Aubrey announced that she was the most popular girl in fourth grade, which might be true but shouldn't be. It's true only because when it comes to popularity, pretty matters more than whether anyone actually likes you.

I continue to wave, imitating Aubrey now. I say, "I am the most popular girl in the world."

"Ugh," you say. "Shoot me if I ever become like that."

I stop waving and look at you. "I'd never shoot you," I say.

"Well, *do* something, *okay?*"

"But you'd never be like Aubrey," I say.

"Yeah, but just in case. Send me a signal. Like a secret message."

"What kind of message?" I imagine holding a giant sign that says DON'T BE LIKE THAT.

"Something. I don't know. Make it big. Something that really gets my attention."

I shrug. "Okay."

"Like, in a major way. Make it serious."

I think about that for a bit. I'm not sure exactly what you mean, but I like the idea of a secret message, some code understood only by you and me. I say, simply, "Sure, it's a deal."

When the song ends, you say into your hairbrush microphone, "Introducing... the great... Mizz Frizz!!!"

I wrinkle my nose. "Mizz Frizz?"

"Yeah," you say. "Because of your hair." You press *Play,* and on comes a song I love so much, one my mother used to play for me. It's about waking up surrounded by ten *million fireflies, which is something I like to imagine. Ten million fireflies blinking on and off around my head, as if all the distant stars had come down to Earth just to say hello.*

"I love this song!" I say.

"I know, dummy," you answer.

I hop on the bed and belt the words toward the ceiling: "'I'd like to make myself belieeeeeve that planet Earth turns slowly...'"

Then you leap up on the bed next to me. I say, "And let's welcome Strawberry Girl, ladies and gentlemen..."

"Strawberry Girl!?"

"Yeah, because of your strawberry-blonde hair."

"Oooh, I love it!"

Then you sing into that hairbrush, "''Cause everything is never as it seems...'"

One of your arms is stretched out wide, and your chin is tilted upward. Your eyes are almost entirely closed, and your lips are pulled into a smile.

You look so happy.

I say to you then, "My mom says when she sells that big house on Laura Lane, she'll take us out to the House of Gasho." The House of Gasho is a restaurant where chefs cook the food on the table right in front of you.

"Cool," you say. You are still swaying to the beat.

There is a knock on the door, and before we can scramble off the bed, your mom pops her head in.

"Girls," your mom says. Her voice is serious, but her face looks like she's trying not to smile. "Aren't you supposed to be doing homework?"

"We took a break," you answer. You are standing frozen in a kind of rock-star position, leaned over toward the hairbrush.

"Well," says your mom. She is smiling now, for real. "Maybe it's time to take a break from your break."

"Okay," you say.

"Okay," I say.

She winks at us and closes the door.

We turn the music off, and suddenly we are back to being Franny and Suzy, just regular kids instead of rock stars. We pick our books back up and return to Ma-Jell-O, to de Soda, to Captain James Cook and his restaurant for kangaroos.

experts #2 & #3

I'D NEVER HAVE GUESSED HOW MANY PEOPLE spent their lives thinking about jellyfish. And not just biologists, either. There were NASA engineers who studied jellies' jet propulsion. Performers who brought enormous jellyfish puppets to concerts and other events, making the night sky look exactly like the sea. There were researchers who studied jellyfish anatomy. Ecology. Evolution. I took notes on some of them, writing down the most important facts, then folded those pages into the back of my science notebook.

Before one of our labs, I flipped through them. Justin peered over my shoulder. "What's that?"

I quickly shoved them into the back of my notebook and slammed it shut.

"Oh," Justin said. He looked startled. "Sorry, I didn't mean to be nosy. I just—"

Then he started laughing. "I dunno, they looked like FBI notes or something. Are you, like, an undercover agent or something?"

I glared at him.

"Agent Swanson," he said, saluting. "Reporting for duty..."

How was I supposed to respond to that, anyway?

Even if I'd wanted to tell him anything, I still hadn't found the perfect researcher yet.

What I wanted was someone who knew something about stings.

POSSIBLE EXPERT #2:
<u>Diana Nyad, Long-Distance Swimmer</u>
64 years old but not remotely grandmotherly. Actually, she looks like she could punch a champion boxer in the face and walk away unharmed.

Short hair. Very, very muscular.

Has tried four times to swim from Cuba to Florida, but each time had to stop because she'd been stung so badly by jellyfish. There are photographs of her online, her face blistered and swollen beyond recognition.

She is training for a fifth attempt now. She is practicing by swimming in the Caribbean for up to twenty hours a day.

Advantages:

- Firsthand expertise with stings.
- Looks tough.
- Like, really tough.
- It might be good to have someone so tough helping me.

Disadvantages:

- Twenty hours a day? That will make conversation difficult.

- That means after swimming, she has just four hours left over for everything else. Not certain that would be enough time to help me.
- Do I really want to know what a jellyfish sting feels like?
- She looks so tough, I wonder if she's even nice.

Conclusion:

- Temporarily rejected, because frankly I am a little frightened of the woman. But watch her. She's interesting.

POSSIBLE EXPERT #3:
Angel Yanagihara,
Biochemist in Hawaii

When she was a young woman, she was stung by a box jellyfish, which is related to the Irukandji. Barely made it to shore before blacking out. Frankly, she is lucky to be alive. Since then she developed the first-ever treatment for a jellyfish sting. She is currently helping that 64-year-old swimmer, Diana Nyad, figure out how to swim from Cuba to Florida without letting the jellyfish stop her again.

Long, straight blondish hair. Almost strawberry blonde, actually.

Advantages:

- Box jellyfish are very similar to the Irukandji.
- Knows all about stings.
- Created her own treatment for jellyfish stings.
- She understands about fixing things. About making things right.
- She is pretty. Long, straight blonde hair and sparkly eyes.
- Maybe even reminds me a little bit of Franny?
- Perhaps that is a sign.

<u>Disadvantages:</u>
- ??

<u>Conclusion:</u>
- Maybe this is the one? Research more.

I couldn't stop looking at Angel's picture. She had long, flat blonde hair, almost like Franny's. She knew everything a person would need to know to really help me.

It was practically perfect. And I almost picked her. I swear I did.

But then I found a video of her online, a clipping from a news show about her work. The video showed her injecting a mouse with venom from a box jellyfish—the same kind that had stung her. She taped the mouse belly-up to a table in her laboratory, shaved his fur off, then watched on a monitor as the mouse came nearer and nearer to death. She didn't even wince.

I knew how it felt to inflict pain, then stand there and watch. I'd done it before.

So it didn't matter to me that Angel Yanagihara was doing it for a good cause, or even that she swooped in at the last minute with her treatment. I wanted to stay as far from this woman as possible.

It turns out she didn't remind me of Franny after all. She reminded me of *me*.

And then I saw Jamie, and I knew. Jamie was the one.

how to not say something important

I AM SITTING ON THE MORNING SCHOOL BUS. *I
have been thinking about a book we are reading in
fifth grade, about a dog named after a supermarket and
a girl who makes friends with an old lady who had too
much alcohol in her life. In the book, the old lady hangs
empty bottles from a tree to remind her of all her mis-
takes. When bottles knock together in the breeze, they
sound like chimes, and that is my favorite thing about
this book: the image of those dangling bottles, all those
terrible memories that somehow make music when they
knock against one another.*

You see, I have my own terrible memory now, one I

haven't told you about yet. That terrible memory is this: My mom and dad told me they are getting a divorce.

They told me over dinner at Elmer Suds Pub, which is the place with the curly fries and the tables that are so tall you need to sit on barstools. My mom said she helped my dad find a new apartment—"a perk of being in real estate, I guess"—and they both laughed, which frankly I thought was weird.

I am going to be one of those kids with divorced parents.

It's bad enough that Aaron had to leave, that he is off at college having all kinds of adventures without us. It's as if all the loneliness he left behind in the house just cracked the rest of our family in half.

I want so badly to tell you. It is the biggest news I have ever had.

But every time I've tried to tell you, I haven't been able to make the words come.

You get on the bus and walk toward me, toward the seat we always sit in. And I think: Maybe now. Maybe now is the time.

But when you sit down, your eyes are dancing, and

you look like you have something you want to talk about. You don't even say hello. Instead, you whisper to me, "Who do you like?"

I don't know what to say. Even if that were the thing I wanted to talk about, there are lots of possible answers. I like Fluffernutter. I like you. I like Aaron. I like my mom and dad, even if I am mad at them for getting divorced. I like the woodpecker that knocks against the tree outside my window. I like the moon when it's a thin crescent and looks like a cartoon drawing of a closed eye, as if the sky were winking.

"What?"

"Boys, I mean. Who do you like?"

I wrinkle my nose. I say, "No one." Which I know is what girls say when they don't want to tell people who they like, but in this case, it is true. I don't like anyone. Not like that.

You frown at me, and I feel the chance to tell you about my parents slipping away.

"But you have to like someone," you say. "We'll be in middle school soon."

I turn those words over in my brain. I have to?

There are some things I have to do; I know this. I have to eat. I have to drink water. I have to breathe. But beyond those things, it doesn't seem like there's anything else on Earth that I really have to do, even the things my mom says I must—things like clearing the table, or showering more now that I'm getting older.

Still, I don't say these words aloud. I know that if I say them, you will roll your eyes. You've started doing that lately, and, frankly, I don't like it one bit.

From the back of the bus, I hear a group of boys laughing, the way boys do when they are in a big group.

So I ask, "Well, who do you like?" It comes out sounding a bit like an accusation.

"I like Dylan," you say, and you blush.

Well, that about floors me.

"Dylan!?" I whisper. "Dylan Parker!?"

You blush deeper now. "Yeah. Dylan Parker."

"Tell me you're kidding." And I know I don't sound very kind when I say that, but this doesn't exactly seem like the sort of thing I should have to be kind about. Nobody should have to be kind about Dylan Parker, because Dylan Parker himself is not kind.

You shrug, almost apologetically. "I just think he's cute."

And that's when I know: Everything is about to change. It's about to get knotted up in the worst possible ways.

I think about my hair, about the tangles I battle every morning. I have spent so many hours of my life trying to brush out tangles. But no matter how carefully I try to pull the individual strands apart, they just get tighter and tighter. They cinch together in all the worst ways, until they are impossible to straighten out. Sometimes there is nothing to be done but to get out a pair of scissors and cut the knot right out.

But how do you cut out a knot that's formed by people?

I don't like where this is going at all.

crazy brave

J AMIE IS NOT WHAT YOU MIGHT THINK. HE'S not how you might imagine the hero of a story.

He is old, first of all. Not as old as Diana Nyad, maybe. But at least as old as my dad, and my dad is going to be fifty next year.

He looks like a dad, too. He has lines around his eyes and on his forehead, and his lower jaw is tucked under the rest of his face like a drawer that's been pushed in a teeny bit too far. There are lots of gray hairs on his head, and when he wears what he calls his stinger suit—a nylon wet suit that protects him from jellyfish stings—he kind of looks like a toddler wearing tight pajamas.

Jamie—Dr. Jamie Seymour, professor of biology—works in a lab at James Cook University in Cairns, which is a city in Queensland, which is a state in Australia, which is both the world's largest island and the world's smallest continent.

In Australia, people have seen spiders eat birds, centipedes eat snakes, snakes eat crocodiles, crocodiles eat children. There are killer ants that lunge at humans. An octopus that contains enough venom to kill twenty-six humans. Birds with such terrible claws they sometimes rip the insides right out of full-grown people.

You have to be crazy brave to live in Australia.

I watched a lot of videos of Jamie. In the first video I saw him in, Jamie jumped into water that was swarming with deadly jellyfish—I'm talking about jellyfish that could kill him in three minutes flat—like it was nothing at all.

Jamie grabbed one of those jellyfish with his bare

hands. Ten feet of tentacles swirled all around. All casual, he told a TV reporter that the jellyfish he was holding contained enough venom to kill fifteen humans.

I could see how nervous the reporter was. The reporter tried to smile nonchalantly. He cracked a joke, as if saying, *Ha-ha, yeah, all part of the job.* But I could see the way he leaned back, away from the animal, and couldn't really think of what to say.

I could see the fear in his eyes.

In another video, Jamie got into the water, and even though he was covered head to toe in a stinger suit, there was just a tiny little part of his face that was exposed. That was all it took. He was brushed on the lower lip, ever so slightly, like a kiss from a tentacle he never even saw.

He was brushed on the lip by an Irukandji.

An actual Irukandji.

Jamie had been filming for a television show when it happened, and they caught the whole thing on camera. I watched their report of the incident.

After Jamie was stung, he writhed in pain for two

full days, which is almost three thousand minutes. When I calculated that, I tried pinching myself as hard as I could for exactly sixty seconds.

Try that, and then multiply it, if you can, by three thousand, and you still won't have even the slightest sense of what Jamie went through. The whole time, Jamie lay on a hospital bed, wearing only a red bathing suit. He cried, he curled into a ball, he vomited. He knew the cameras were on him, and he let them record it all.

Later, Jamie said that as he lay in that hospital, he was convinced he was going to die.

He wasn't like Angel Yanagihara, who stung a mouse, then watched as it got closer and closer to death.

He *was* the mouse.

The weirdest part of the whole video came after he was out of the hospital, though. Because as soon as he felt better—like, the very instant—he got right back into the water. Just like that, he went back to those jellyfish. He laughed and joked, as if those two days hadn't even happened. He didn't even seem mad.

And that's one of the reasons I liked him. I liked him because he had been stung and it hadn't changed him.

He had a sense of humor. He was fearless. He could forgive.

Best of all, it seemed like Jamie was the one person who was crazy enough not to think *I* was crazy.

I felt certain he could help me prove that *sometimes things just happen* isn't actually a reason for anything.

And if he could help me with this, he'd be helping with something else, too. He'd be helping me write a new ending, a better ending, to the story of my friendship with Franny.

An ending in which I'm one of the good guys. Not the villain.

part four

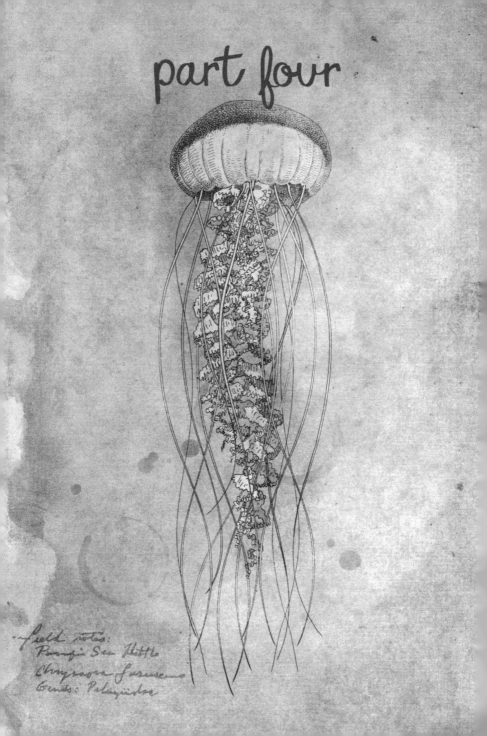

field notes:
Pacific Sea Nettle
Chrysaora fuscescens
Genus: Pelagiidae

Variables

Scientists are ultimately exploring cause and effect—how changes to one part of the world can cause other things to change. But cause and effect are not always easy to measure. So well-designed research studies will have clearly defined variables—independent, dependent, and controlled—that help scientists identify what's changing and what's causing the change.

—MRS. TURTON

blooms

T HE NEXT THING I WANT TO TELL YOU ABOUT
jellyfish is this: They are taking over.

Did you know that? Not many people do. It's our own fault, but no one is even paying attention. People pay attention to other things. They pay attention to videos of cats playing pianos, or to which movie star is in rehab, or to who stole who else's boyfriend. They pay attention to shades of eye shadow and online games and which angle makes them look best in photos.

But meanwhile. Out there in the sea. Jellyfish blooms are on the rise.

Isn't that a pretty phrase? *Jellyfish blooms*, like garden flowers opening up to the sun.

There are more jellyfish than ever. At least, that's what some scientists say.

People are the problem. We take other fish from the ocean—too many fish. We send them to factories and press them into breaded sticks and patties. We truck them to Red Lobster and Long John Silver's. We fill supermarket cases with their flesh, all slick and gleaming on heaps of ice.

When we do these things, jellyfish blooms grow bigger. Jellies have less competition for their foods now. They grow in number, move in massive groups, devouring everything.

The seas are warming, which is terrible for almost everyone. They are also filling with chemicals. Huge sections of the seas today dont't have enough oxygen. But jellyfish love a warm ocean, the chemicals don't hurt jellyfish one bit, and they carry all the oxygen they need right inside their watery selves.

There are now so many jellyfish that power plants around the world have been shut down when hundreds of thousands of the creatures have clogged their seawater cooling systems. Jellyfish populations are getting so huge, they are stealing the food supply from animals you'd never expect—even penguins in Antarctica. One scientist believes they might some-day starve whales to extinction.

Nobody knows this. Nobody thinks about it or talks about it. I mean, this is some of the biggest news around, and when was the last time you even *saw* a jellyfish on television?

But they're out there, I'm telling you.

They are out there right this second. They are moving silently, endlessly, all of them, through the darkness of the sea.

how to drift apart

*E*VERYTHING CHANGES. IT STARTS CHANGING *almost instantly after you tell me you like Dylan Parker, and by the summer before sixth grade, it is all different.*

The first thing I notice is the way you tug at your clothing. You might put on a dress that's just a little short, which isn't a big deal on its own. Except then you seem to spend the rest of the day thinking about it. I can tell you're thinking about it, too, because you keep touching your hem. You tug at it, pull it down, like maybe you have decided you actually want to cover your knees after all. Or you just keep smoothing the dress out, over and over, even though it looks exactly the same before and after.

And all that tugging and all that smoothing makes me think about your dress, too, wondering if it is too short or just right.

That is what bothers me most. Because I don't want to think about your dress. There are so many other things to think about. Important things.

Months have passed now, and I still haven't told you. I still haven't told you about my parents.

I want to. I want to invite you over to my dad's new apartment, show you the big television he just got, which is exactly the kind of thing my mother would have called "a waste of good money." I want you to see the way my mom spread her stuff into his side of the closet, how it looks like his suits were never even hanging there in the first place.

But every time I start to say something, you are busy smoothing your dress or looking in the mirror. You look in every mirror, any mirror, no matter where we are. I won't even realize there is a mirror there until I see you eyeing yourself from different positions.

Once you see yourself in that mirror, whatever conversation we were having is over.

"I hate my hair," you say, smoothing down a portion of your bangs. I don't understand what's to hate about your hair. I'm the one whose curly hair won't smooth down, and if I don't mind mine, there is no reason at all you should mind yours.

But then you start worrying about my hair, too.

"You know," you say, and I think you are trying to be helpful, "I'll bet with the right product, we could actually make your hair look almost cute."

Cute. *You use that word all the time now.*

"Omigosh," you might say. "I saw the cutest pair of Chuck Taylors at the mall."

"Who's Chuck Taylor?" I ask. I imagine tiny look-alike toddlers in baggy pants—Little Chuck 1 and Little Chuck 2.

"No, dummy," you say, rolling your eyes. "Chuck Taylors are super-cute sneakers. Don't you know anything?"

I do know things. I know lots of things. I just don't happen to know very much about types of shoes, that's all.

I know, for example, that time and space are the same thing, and that it is possible that all moments in time exist simultaneously, which means I am just born and a kid and an old lady and just plain dead and have never even existed, all at the same moment, right now.

I know that everything exists because tiny specks, too small to see, move through an invisible field the way a pair of boots moves through mud, getting heavier as they go.

And since my parents split up, I have begun to wonder if this is happening to me, too: if I am getting more weighed down, harder to lift, as I move through this world.

Anyway, you don't seem to care about the things I know. Not anymore. You once wanted me to tell you everything, and now you care only about Chuck Taylors and the hem of your dress and whatever it is you see when you look in the mirror.

Which makes me wonder this: If you care about things I don't understand, and you don't care about the things I do understand, what will we have to talk about anymore?

I don't buy any "product" for my hair.

After a while, you buy it for me—some sort of clear, sticky gel that smells like bad perfume. You rub it in with your fingers, then blow-dry my hair. But that only makes my hair extra-frizzy, as if I stuck a finger in an electric socket.

"Hmm." You frown. "You really do have impossible hair."

And that's when I want to say this: Maybe. Maybe I do have impossible hair, and maybe that's a bad thing, but I never thought about it until right this very minute.

That's when I remember the thing you said once.

You said, "Shoot me if I ever become like that."

You said, "Send me a signal . . . a secret message."

You said, "Make it big."

But I don't know what the right signal is, the message that would say: I want you to care again about the things I care about.

I don't know how to say: I used to like myself when I was around you, but now I'm not so sure.

I don't know how to say: Please, please don't be another thing that changes.

So I don't say anything. I just let you add a different product to my electrifrizzy hair until it looks like I rubbed my head in a tub of Vaseline. Then after you go home, I wash it all out.

Around that same time, Aaron comes home for dinner. He brings his new friend, Rocco, and Mom makes everyone twice-baked potatoes and smiles too much. For some reason, she is acting as if Aaron has brought home, like, Elvis Presley himself. Like there is something that makes this friend very different from any of Aaron's other friends who have come for dinner.

While we eat, I tell them about you, about the way you're always looking in the mirror and I don't know what to talk to you about.

"Oh, that's just a phase girls go through," says Mom, waving her hand. She laughs a little too loudly; then she stands up to clear our plates.

But Aaron watches me closely.

"Maybe," he says. "I hope it's a phase, anyway. But, kiddo, I gotta warn you: You're entering some hard years."

He glances at Rocco, who shakes his head. "Middle school," Rocco says in response. "You couldn't pay me to go back to middle school."

a click, then silence

I PLANNED TO REACH OUT TO JAMIE BY E-MAIL. BUT the first time I tried, I just sat there looking at the blinking cursor until my butt hurt from all the sitting.

Better, I thought, to write my ideas down on paper first. But even then, I couldn't find the words and kept scratching out what I'd written.

I tried being formal:

Dear Mr. Seymour:
Dear Dr. Seymour:

But that didn't feel right. So I tried the opposite approach:

Hi, Jamie:
· Greetings! You don't know me, but...

I tried by opening politely:

I am writing on a matter that ~~I need~~
~~your help with~~ requires your ~~knowledge~~
expertise.

I tried being direct:

Jamie, I need your help.

I tried a bunch of different ways, but I couldn't make the words come. Not the way I wanted. I put the pen down and clicked, again, to that video of him getting stung by the Irukandji.

I tried explaining the background:

I have a ~~friend~~ classmate who recently
~~died passed~~ perished due to drowning.
The thing is, she was ~~a very good~~
an outstanding swimmer. She died in

Maryland in August. It doesn't really make sense that she could just drown. She really, really was a good swimmer from the very first moment I saw her. Plus, I ~~discovered~~ ~~researched~~ read that the beaches in Maryland don't even have very big waves.

And I even tried to show him how much I'd learned on my own:

I have read recently that jellyfish blooms are expanding all over the world. And that the Irukandji, in particular, which is the type that stung you (I'm sorry if this is ~~painful~~ difficult for you to think about), is likely moving all over the globe. At one time, ~~people~~ experts thought that the Irukandji was found only in Australia, near you. But did you know that Irukandji syndrome was reported in Florida almost ~~ten~~ ~~years~~ a decade ago? Doctors wrote

about it in a ~~magazine~~ medical journal.
I found the article online and will be
happy to ~~send~~ forward it to ~~you~~ your
attention if you would like to see it.

I tried asking questions:

So what I am thinking is this: What
if my ~~friend~~ classmate ~~had been~~ was
stung by a jellyfish? Would we even
know? Would anyone even be looking
for that?

    I mean, is there any way to prove
that the reason she drowned <u>wasn't</u>
because of the Irukandji? How can
anyone ever be sure?

    And if we don't know it happened
to her, how can we prevent it from
happening to someone else?

After I'd watched the video so many times I knew
it by heart, I decided to try another approach.
    I waited until after my mother went to bed.

It was late. Almost midnight.

But Cairns, Australia, is fifteen hours ahead of South Grove, Massachusetts. It would be early afternoon there. In Cairns, they were already living in tomorrow.

I dialed the number I found on the university website. I listened to the phone ring, then heard a crisp woman's voice say, "James Cook Center for Biodiversity, can I help you?"

I opened my mouth to speak, but no sound came out.

Just ask for Jamie, I told myself. I squeezed my eyes shut. *Just ask.*

But I already anticipated what her next question would be. Something like "What is this regarding?" Or "May I ask what this is about?"

And I wasn't quite sure how I could answer that.

"Hello?" she asked. "Is anyone there?"

I pressed the phone against my ear. *I want Jamie's help,* I thought. *I want him to help me do something. For my friend. My friend, my not-friend, who is dead. I want him to help me make sense of that, to explain it, to help me prove that when things like this happen, they happen for a reason.*

I want him to restore some order to this world.

"Hello? Hello?"

In the movies, there's always a dial tone almost immediately after someone hangs up on you. But in real life, there's just a click, then silence. If you're on a cell phone, you might hear a short beep, have a message appear that the call has ended. But if you're in your mother's living room, and it's almost midnight, all you hear is a single click.

Then maybe you hear some creaking from the baseboard heaters before they turn on. And after that, there is silence. Nothing but silence.

Finding the right words has never been a strength of mine.

how to get things wrong

*B*Y THE TIME WE ARE IN SIXTH GRADE, AT THE *Eugene Field Memorial Middle School, every-thing is different.*

It's bigger than our old school, first of all. Three different elementary schools feed into the Eugene Field Memorial Middle School, so there are many strangers. The building is bigger, too, and there are lots of different wings—the sixth-grade wing, the seventh-grade wing, the eighth-grade wing, the arts wing, the phys ed wing. I get lost too often and end up walking the halls with kids who are much older than I am.

And then there are the lockers. Last year, everyone had wooden cubbies, and everything was out in the open.

Now we have cold metal lockers that can only be opened with combinations, all our things hidden from light. The lockers fill entire hallways, entire wings, one after another. At night, I dream I'm walking down those hallways. In my dreams they go on forever.

In middle school, kids cast sideways glances at one another, like they're suspicious of one another. I can see clumps of kids forming—pretty Aubrey with dark hair has started sitting with a pretty girl named Molly who has blonde hair, and they surround themselves with other pretty girls, Anna and Jenna and some others, some of whom I know from elementary school and some of whom I don't. I don't like walking past them when they cluster around lockers together. Their hair is so flat, like they know exactly what product to use, and that makes me conscious of my own wild tangles of hair. It makes me feel like a separate species altogether.

For the first part of the year, lunchtime, at least, is the same as last year, with you and me sitting together and sharing snacks and everything being easy.

But after a while, things change. I don't notice the changes at first.

Each day, I sit down at our regular table and eat my cheese sandwich and wait while you buy your milk. I begin to wait longer than usual. That's because instead of coming straight to the table, you linger. You talk to people, people I don't even know, and you take your time. You aren't just talking, either. You are also standing with a hip stuck out, which makes me wonder if you are waiting for Dylan to walk past. Each day, it seems like you linger a little longer.

Then one day you leave the lunch line, and I think you are walking toward our table. But you don't. Instead, you sit down at a table with other girls. And not just any girls: You sit with Aubrey and Molly and Jenna and Anna. They smile at you like it is totally normal that you would sit there. I can see your mouths moving as you talk.

I meet your eyes from across the room. I frown at you, lift my hands to say, What are you doing?

At first you look away. I don't stop staring at you. After a while, you look back at me. You smile and wave me over.

As if I might want to sit with that group.

I scowl. I look down at my sandwich. A lunch monitor walks past and says to me, "Careful, or your face will freeze in that position."

That night, I tell my mom I want to start buying milk and a snack in the cafeteria. That way, I can stand right next to you as you buy your milk.

The next day, as soon as we have both paid the lunch lady, I say, "Come on," and I pull you toward our regular table.

You come with me, you sit with me, and it is just the two of us like it should be. But you're very quiet for the rest of lunch, and after you eat, you crumple your wrappers and stand without even looking at me.

A few days later, you say, "I'm going to eat with those guys today," and you gesture with your head to Aubrey's table as if it is nothing at all. Your voice is the kind of voice my mother sometimes calls "snippy." After a few seconds, you add, "You should come, too. They're nice." And your voice is a little kinder then, like maybe you feel a little bit sorry.

I follow you to the table. You sit down next to Jenna.

There is not much space, but I squeeze another chair between you anyway. Everyone says hi, but then barely anyone says anything to me for the rest of lunch.

Before lunch ends, the girls bring out little round mirrors. They share blush and eye shadow in various shades of green and blue and gray. They talk about face shape and skin tone, and they point out a bunch of kids who are wearing the wrong colors for their complexions. Somehow you know what they are talking about, know enough to agree that Dorrie Perkins is "olive-y and oval," but that Emma Strank has cool skin tones and a heart-shaped face.

You turn to me and say softly, "Your face is kind of heart-shaped, too, Suzy." And I cannot help it. I make a face at you. You turn away quickly.

The next day, you sit with them again. I follow, because best friends always eat together. Molly is saying that during her hip-hop dance class, she wraps her legs and stomach in plastic wrap. This way, she sweats more.

I think about the advice my mother has always given

me: that it's important to ask other people lots of questions. So I ask, "Why would you want to sweat more, anyway?"

Molly doesn't answer, but Aubrey leans over to me and says, very slowly, as if it is obvious, "It makes her pants fit better."

I try again.

"Actually, humans have the most sweat glands on the bottom of their feet." I say this because it's true, and also because it's joining the conversation.

Molly looks at me and raises a single eyebrow. That's how I know I said the wrong thing.

I try again. "Did you know that sweat is sterile when it comes out of your body?"

Molly presses her lips together, and her nostrils flare ever so slightly.

"It's kind of like pee," I say. "Everybody thinks pee is so gross, but it's actually totally clean."

The table gets very, very still.

"Some people even drink their own pee, you know."

I notice that Jenna's hand, which had been about to put a piece of popcorn in her mouth, is frozen in midair.

Jenna looks at Molly. Aubrey looks at you, then at Anna. Nobody looks at me.

I say, "Most of the time, when people drink their pee, it's because they have to. Like because they're trapped under rubble or something. But some people do it because they think it's good for them."

Jenna shakes her head, puts the piece of popcorn down. Molly closes her eyes and presses her lips together. It looks like she is trying not to laugh.

Actually, it looks like everyone is trying not to laugh. Even you.

"Oh, and you know who else drinks their pee?" I cannot seem to stop the words from coming, even though I realize, even as they're coming out, that they're the wrong ones.

"Butterflies. They get salts and minerals that way. And a lot of animals use pee to communicate with each other. I mean, I know that sounds pretty gross...but..." When my voice trails off, I bite my lip. I take a few deep breaths, try to ignore the silence.

I reach into my bag and pull out my Fruit Roll-Up. It's strawberry-flavored.

I offer it to you. "Want this?"

You shake your head. You do not look at me.

I say, "You sure? It's strawberry-*flavored...."*

You gaze past me, your eyes focused on something just above my right shoulder.

I say, "Get it?"

The other girls meet one another's eyes again.

"Strawberry for Strawberry Girl," I offer again, waving the Fruit Roll-Up slightly.

Your eyes snap right back at me then. They narrow.

"Huh?" asks Aubrey.

"Nothing," you snap. "It's nothing. Just something stupid we did when we were really, really little." You shoot me a fierce look.

"Some people don't know when it's time to grow up, that's all," you add.

You stand. And just like that, the other girls stand, too.

Just before you stride away, you lean down to me, so close I can feel your heat. Your face is flushed red. Your eyes are blazing. "Why do you have to be so weird, Suzy?" you hiss.

I have never seen you this angry. And I am confused,

because all I did was offer you my Fruit Roll-Up, which is something friends do.

"You're just. So. Weird," you say. You turn away from me and storm out of the cafeteria. The other girls follow.

And I'm so amazed—as amazed as I was that first day I met you, when I saw you unexpectedly swim underwater, back when I thought you were like me and you couldn't swim.

Those girls are following you. You are the girl who was once afraid to read aloud in class, afraid to spend the night away from your mother, and now these girls are following you.

No one even turns around to glance back at me.

face-to-face

A T THE BEGINNING OF EACH SESSION, DR. LEGS asked me just one question: "Would you prefer silence or speaking today?" Each week, I responded the same way: I pressed my lips together and stared at my feet.

Dr. Legs leaned back in her chair, clasped her hands in her lap, and met my silence with her own. As my parents waited on the other side of the door, we sat wordless, week after week.

Which made me think about a musician Aaron once told me about: a composer who wrote a piece with no notes whatsoever. When the piece is performed, a musician comes onstage, opens the piano, sets a timer, and plays nothing. Aaron said the first time the piece was performed, the audience got nervous—they whispered to one another and shifted in their seats, and some even walked out. Now when it's performed, people expect the silence. Instead of getting mad or nervous, they hear other things: the rustling of programs, fabric sliding against seats, polite coughing. They hear *themselves*, which they wouldn't hear otherwise, even though those noises are always there.

That piece is called *4'33"*, because the performer sits quietly for exactly four minutes and thirty-three seconds.

If people were silent, they could hear the noise of their own lives better. If people were silent, it would make what they did say, whenever they chose to say it, more important. If people were silent, they could read one another's signals, the way underwater creatures flash lights at one another, or turn their skin different colors.

Humans are so bad at reading one another's signals. I knew this by now.

Sometimes I tried to imagine what signals Dr. Legs was sending me, but I couldn't tell. I'd lived in the world of words for so long, I guess, that silence still wasn't a language I understood.

Each week, after forty-five minutes, Dr. Legs ended the silence by saying, "Okay, time's up."

I sure hoped my parents weren't spending a whole lot of money for these sessions.

During my fourth session with Dr. Legs, something changed. About halfway through the appointment, Dr. Legs spoke.

"Suzanne," she said, "I wonder if you have ever given much thought to why people speak to one another. Why speech came about in the first place."

Dr. Legs explained that many people believe spoken communication evolved because human societies had become so complex that hand gestures and grunting were no longer enough.

Then she added, "But that's not what I believe."

If she thought I was going to ask what she believed, she was wrong.

Dr. Legs leaned in toward me and said, "I think it developed from our need to be understood."

Our need to be understood. Those words made me think of all the things I'd done wrong to make Franny understand—everything that had happened leading up to the moment when I saw her walking away from me for the last time, crying and carrying those awful bags.

It hurt too much to think about, so I pushed the memory out of my brain as quickly as I could. Just like I always did.

Instead, I thought about Jamie. Since my failed phone call, I'd been thinking hard about how to reach him.

"Being understood is a fundamental human need," Dr. Legs said. "Wouldn't you like to be better understood?"

I sat very still. *Trust me*, Dr. Legs had said in our first session. *I won't judge.*

But how could this woman, of all people, help anyone understand me?

"Isn't there something you desperately want to express?"

Well, yes. I needed Jamie's help. So I nodded.

"Perhaps I can help you find the words," she said. Her voice was low and excited, as if she and I were partners in some great conspiracy.

I could tell she thought we were experiencing the kind of thing she would probably call a *breakthrough*.

I narrowed my eyes to let her know this was no breakthrough.

"Well," she said, "whatever you want to say, I recommend you come right out and say it. Just open your mouth and tell the world what's on your mind."

Jamie, help me, I thought. *Jamie, you are the one.*

"Of course, with your generation," she continued, "I always feel like I have to add this: Please don't do it through text or e-mail or anything like that. When you need to communicate something important, speak your truth *face-to-face*."

Face-to-face. Ha. The person I needed help from was literally on the other side of the world.

"There's a *reason* I'm saying this, Suzanne," Dr. Legs said. "Did you know that most of what we communicate to other people is nonverbal?"

Some of us try to communicate without words, anyway, I thought. *It doesn't always work.*

It sure didn't work for me.

"When you say what you have to say through a computer or a phone, there are often *miscommunications.* But when it's *just you and someone else,* and you're *right in front of them,* speaking *your truth,* they are much more likely to *understand.*"

Just me. Speaking my truth. Face-to-face.

"And I'll bet you anything they'll respond."

I imagined myself sitting across from Jamie. He was smiling at me, as if asking, *Can I help you?*

I smiled back.

Dr. Legs said, "I see you smiling. So that helps you, I hope?"

I shrugged, which she apparently took to mean yes.

"*Wonderful,*" she said. She sat back, folding her arms across her belly. "Just *wonderful.*"

We sat in silence for the rest of the session. When Dr. Legs opened the door, she smiled broadly at my parents. "I think we made *major headway* today," she said to them.

They grinned back at her, all big hopes and open hearts.

millions of things to learn

I THOUGHT A LOT ABOUT JAMIE AS I RESEARCHED jellyfish for my science report. It was hard to imagine how anybody could ever become an expert in jellies. There were millions and millions of things to learn—more than I ever imagined a person *could* learn about a single animal.

For example, if you cut a jellyfish in half, it might just become two jellyfish; they can divide in the same way cells do. And if you injure a jellyfish, you might find hundreds of little clones floating about, tiny replicas generated one after another from the damaged tissue, as if spit out from a 3-D printer.

There were more than 1,500 species of jellyfish...
maybe even as many as 10,000. We were discovering new things about them all the time. The thought
of it made me dizzy—like I could study jellyfish for
the rest of my life and never run out of new things to
learn.

As I worked, Dr. Legs's words kept echoing in my
head.

*When you need to communicate something important,
speak your truth face-to-face.*

I wanted to. I wanted to sit down with Jamie so
badly. With each new fact I learned—*box jellies have
primitive eyes, even though they don't have a brain*—I
wanted to sit with him even more.

If I could sit down with Jamie, he could tell me
all the things I'd never think to ask on my own—
things about ocean currents, and water temperatures,
and what we know about where Irukandji syndrome
has shown up in the world. Maybe he would plug all
sorts of numbers into a spreadsheet and then say, *"Yes.
Yes, you are right, Suzy Swanson. You figured out what
happened to your friend. You are the only one who did."*

If I could sit down with Jamie, I'd tell him things, too. I'd tell him about a biologist I read about, someone who lived a long time ago: He was walking on a beach soon after his wife died. He saw a jellyfish in a tide pool, and the swirl of the tentacles reminded him of the swirl of her hair, and then he spent the rest of his life painting pictures of jellyfish.

I would tell Jamie all about Franny—about how she was here, and then she was not, and how I saw the swirl of her hair inside those tanks.

Meeting Jamie would be impossible. It would mean flying to a different continent, which would be insane. *Cray cray*, as Franny would say. It couldn't in a million years happen.

But what if it could?

how to know
things have changed

*A*FTER THE DAY AT LUNCH WHEN *I* TALK ABOUT
*pee, I keep my mouth shut. I sit at the table with
you and those girls, but I don't say anything.*

Nobody says anything to me, either.

*A few weeks go by like that: I sit down and watch
the rest of you talk. Then one day, I sit back down at our
old table. You don't join me, and when you sit with those
other girls, your back is to me.*

*Weeks go by. Then a month. I read books while I eat.
I do homework. I listen to the noises in the cafeteria—
the clamor of kids, the slam of lockers, the crumpling of
brown paper bags, the shouts from lunch monitors: "No*

running," "Pick up your trash, please," "Cafeteria trays are not to be used as weapons, please."

I wait for you to come back.

We don't see each other on weekends anymore. If I call, you tell me you and your mom are shopping together. Or you're visiting your great-aunt Lynda. You have a math tutor, because factorials are really confusing to you.

One day, an unusually warm day in spring, I get an idea: I will ride my bike to your house. I will apologize for being weird at lunch, for talking about how pee is sterile. I'll promise not to be weird anymore, if we can just start over.

I have lived for eleven and a half years, which is 4,199 days if you include two leap years, and that is 100,776 hours, which is over six million minutes, but only on planet Earth.

On Pluto, which takes almost 250 Earth years to revolve around the sun, I would still be a year old. On Mercury, on the other hand, I would be forty-five.

But on Earth, I am eleven and a half, and that is old enough to not be weird.

I stop my bicycle on the sidewalk across from your house. I hear voices. Girls' voices.

There are three girls in the yard, and they are spraying each other with a hose. And they look almost like teenagers, the way they are squealing in the wet spray. I watch for a while, until one of them, the one with strawberry-blonde hair, seems to look up.

You look just long enough to see me there. Then you turn away, return to squealing.

I become intensely aware of my cutoff shorts, the fact that I'm wearing a faded Hilltown Realty T-shirt— HILLTOWN REALTY: TURNING YOUR DREAMS INTO AN ADDRESS!—the one my mom wears when she's gardening.

I see myself as you just did. As someone who is out of place in this world.

zombie ants

THE TEMPERATURES DROPPED. GIRLS STARTED wearing their jeans tucked into sheepskin boots. Frost appeared on the windows. Mom grumbled about how nobody ever buys a house when the weather gets cold.

Before long, students began presenting science reports in Mrs. Turton's class. A bunch of the science reports were interesting—Molly did her report about scoliosis; she held up X-ray images of her sister's back, showed us how her sister's spine bent in slow curves like a lazy river. Jenna did her report about dolphins, whose hearing, she said, is ten times better than humans'.

Justin did a report on mutated cats. He showed a picture of a cat with two different faces.

"See, Frank and Louie here have two faces, two mouths, two noses, and three eyes," he said. "They even made it into the *Guinness World Records* book!"

Dylan did his about lightning, which was dull, because lightning isn't alive, and besides, all he did was explain what different kinds of lightning looked like.

The reports were scheduled three per day for a week and a half; I was scheduled for the last day. With each presentation, I felt my own getting closer.

Now we are eleven kids away.

Now ten. Now nine.

Now Sarah Johnston was standing in front of the class talking about zombie ants.

"A fungus takes over the ant's brain," she explained. "It begins to control the ant's mind, making it do things that no ant would do otherwise."

Insect mind control. It's a pretty good topic for a report, actually.

"The ant stumbles away from the colony like a

drunk," she continued. "Until now, everything the ant did was for the good of the colony. But not anymore. It goes to a precise location, like it's guided by a GPS. Then it dies, and a stalk starts growing out of the ant's head."

She pointed to a photograph of a desiccated insect with a stick emerging from its corpse—it was gross, but kind of fascinating, too.

"Then one day," she said, "that stalk explodes and sends spores down onto the new colony. So new ants get taken over."

Justin's head had been down on his desk for most of Sarah's presentation, but he lifted it at that comment. "Sounds like middle school," he said dryly.

I saw a flicker of a smile on Sarah's lips, but Mrs. Turton gave Justin a warning look.

"Sarah, I'm curious," Mrs. Turton said. "What made you choose this topic?"

Sarah hesitated. "Well," she said. She bit her lip and thought. "I saw it on a television show. And I just thought it was so cool. But also really, really scary. Like, the idea that something like this could happen—something could just control your brain."

"Does it seem less scary now that you know more about it?"

Sarah shook her head. "No," she said. "It's still scary. But it's still cool. Creepy cool."

Mrs. Turton laughed. "Creepy cool," she said. "I like that. Thanks, Sarah."

As Sarah returned to her seat, the rest of the class applauded politely. Now we were one report closer to mine.

Without knowing why, I opened to the back of my notebook. I began to write.

Jamie, if my report goes well, people will do more than applaud. They'll feel something. They'll feel how I do when I think about how the oceans are changing in all the worst ways, and how jellyfish will starve even whales. I want them to understand that the world is so much bigger than the Eugene Field

Memorial Middle School, and how much there still is to figure out.

Once they understand this, they'll know what a big deal it is when you and I prove what happened to Franny.

I can do it, Jamie.

I think I can do it.

But, oh man, I wish I didn't have to speak in front of the class.

how to lose
a friend

*L*ATE SPRING. WE ARE AT THE SIXTH-GRADE
campout at Rock Lake.

*Our class has done a ropes course and zip line.
We've linked arms and crawled one at a time through
a Hula-Hoop, without breaking arms. We've led one
another, blindfolded, through the twists and turns of
the forest. Girls have run from simple spiders, boys have
tackled one another in the grass. One of our chaperones,
Mr. Andrews, who is a sixth-grade homeroom teacher,
has shown everyone how to build a campfire, starting
with sticks placed in the shape of a teepee. Soon we'll
cook hot dogs and smother them in ketchup, then roast*

marshmallows over the fire until the marshmallows burst into flames and turn black.

On the bus ride here, I sat alone. You walked past my seat and plopped yourself next to Aubrey. If I turned around, I could see your back as you leaned across the aisle to gossip with Jenna.

You and Molly are wearing matching barrettes at the front of your hair, clipped just so. Somehow, those barrettes manage to make you look older, not younger. You're both wearing lip gloss, and in your half-zipped sweatshirts and jeans, you look a little like twins. The boys are running in and out of the woods, throwing sticks and small logs into the fire. The larger logs send sparks up into the air, which makes everyone cheer. Then Justin picks up a stone, lifts it over his head, and hurls it right into the center of the fire. The sparks scatter everywhere, fast, and several girls jump back, screaming.

"Sixth graders, come on over!" Mr. Andrews waves to us from beneath a tree a short distance away. He begins counting down. "Ten, nine, eight..."

The boys dash over, their arms and legs everywhere, tripping and knocking into one another as they go. The girls move more slowly. They walk in a pack, and they don't care that they're not over by Mr. Andrews by the time he finishes counting. I walk close behind those girls—close behind you—but I am not part of your slow-moving, boy-watching group. I am in a different category altogether.

I am becoming an expert in watching other girls' backs.

"Ladies," Mr. Andrews says. "Nice of you to join us."

Then he turns to the group and asks, "What do you hear?" His legs are farther apart than his shoulders. His hair is so short, he's almost bald. He looks like a soldier. Or a pit bull.

Everyone is still. Then Justin Maloney makes a farting noise, and everyone laughs except Mr. Andrews. Aubrey leans over and whispers something in your ear. You giggle.

I wish so badly you would look at me.

Mr. Andrews repeats his question. "What do you hear?"

I close my eyes. I listen. After so many days of sitting alone, listening to the cafeteria noises, I'm good at hearing things. I hear the rustling of classmates. The urgent, high-pitched flutter of cricket wings, the up-and-down melody of songbirds, the first who-whooo of an owl. In the distance, from another campground, I hear somebody belting out "The Star-Spangled Banner." From a different campground, a thud-thud, like a drumbeat from some faraway rock song.

Those birds. There are so many out there calling. Some sound like whistles, and others sound like caw-caw-caws. Some are chattery and some are singsongy. They're different sounds, different birds, but there's a rhythm to them. The crickets and owl, too: They all kind of fit. It's like music, somehow, all those pitches, all that rhythm, weaving in and out.

Then, with a start, I understand something. It is music. I am certain—I mean, I just know—that all these different species are playing together, calling around one another's noises. Each of them has picked a pitch, a pattern, and they are filling in one another's empty spaces.

It's a concert, and I can hear it by listening just right.

I open my eyes. I look right at Mr. Andrews.

"It's an orchestra," I say. The words come out a little breathless.

He cocks his head. "What?"

"An orchestra," I repeat. "Or, I don't know. Not exactly an orchestra, but like one, anyway."

He just stares at me.

"All those noises," I continue. "The birds, or whatever. They're playing together...." But even before the words are out, I see one of his eyebrows go up, and I know that this isn't the answer he was looking for. It's the wrong answer, the very wrongest answer, and now that it's out, I cannot take it back.

I shrug, as if to distance myself from my own words. "I mean, that's kind of what it sounds like, anyway."

"Huh," Mr. Andrews says, but in a way that suggests he isn't really thinking at all about what I just said, not even a little bit. And that is all he needs to say. As if he's given them permission, the kids laugh. All of them. You, too.

Mr. Andrews tells the class what we were supposed to have heard. "While Suzy here listens to Mozart in the trees, I want you to hear something else." He makes a rhythmic gesture with his hands, in time with the thumping bass from the faraway rock song.

Then Mr. Andrews explains that sounds at low frequencies travel farther than sounds at high frequencies, and that is why you can always hear the beat of a drum from a faraway parade sooner than you can hear the rest of the band.

My cheeks burn. I wish I'd thought to point that out instead.

Later, I walk around the campground for a while. Just me. I listen to the orchestra above my head until I hear a commotion down by the pond. Dylan and Kevin O'Connor are throwing something back and forth. I think it might be a stone or a ball, but it has limbs.

It's a frog. They're hurling it back and forth at each other.

Stop.

I think that, although I do not speak.

You stand near Dylan. You watch him. Your hip is sticking out, and you do not take your eyes off him.

Dylan must know you are there, because he catches the

frog and turns right to you. He wiggles the animal in your face a little bit. You squeal, like you're frightened. But also as if you like what he's doing in some way.

He grins and looks at the frog in his hand.

He turns toward a tree.

No, no, no.

It's a birch tree. White bark. It's just a few feet away from him.

Please. Please do not do what I think you are going to do.

He lifts his arm.

I suck in my breath. No.

It is all happening in slow motion now, the way he pulls his arm back, like a major-league pitcher about to throw a fastball.

The tree is right in front of him. There is a smile on his face. He winds his arm back.

He is about to kill something for no reason whatsoever.

The other kids scream and laugh at the same time.

No one is stopping this.

I look right at you then, right in your eyes. You can stop this. I feel almost certain of it.

I say your name—"Franny"—but it comes out in a kind of choke.

You cannot hear me. But you must sense something. You must feel me watching you.

You look up, right at me.

I stare at you, hard. I try to communicate everything I can.

Dylan is doing this for you, *I try to tell you with my eyes.* Please don't let him do this, please don't laugh, please don't encourage him.

His arm is back. It is back so far.

Please. You are the girl who ran with me beneath the bats.

The squeals are even louder now.

I have seen you with Fluffernutter. I have seen you cry when people were cruel.

He holds his arm there, just for a moment.

This is not you. I know you. I know you better than any of these people.

And that is when you narrow your eyes. Ever so slightly. But it is enough.

When you do that, I see something I've never seen

before: a kind of deadness in your eyes. You turn away, toward Dylan. At exactly that moment, he releases the frog.

You laugh and clasp your hand to your mouth like everyone else.

There is a half second where the frog flies through the air—ridiculously, cartoonishly—and then there is a noise, a terrible noise. It is both a thud and a splat, both wet and dry.

It is the worst noise I have ever heard.

And then there is a chorus of "Eew" and "Oh, gross" and "Disgusting," all mixed in with laughter. So much laughter.

I turn away from them, from you, from all of you. I have to breathe deeply to keep myself from throwing up.

I didn't know how to stop it.

I don't know any of the right things. I know about things like bats and glowworms. I know that pee and sweat are sterile, and that before the universe existed there was no color, no sound, no light, no air.

But these things are of no use.

I am supposed to know other things. Like how to clip a barrette to the front of my hair so it looks cute-but-not-babyish. Or how to walk in packs and how to squeal at campfire sparks and how to stand near boys with my hip jutting out.

I am supposed to know the perfect thing to say when later, you walk past me with Jenna and she sneers, "An orchestra," as if orchestra *referred to a clump of maggots crawling over one another at the bottom of a trash can. You laugh and keep walking, and it takes me a moment to even realize that you are laughing about me, about the answer I gave to Mr. Andrews.*

I am supposed to know what to do later on that evening, when I hear other kids whispering and giggling in the dark. I am in my sleeping bag, and the giggles come close, really close, and then I feel someone hovering just above me.

I feel something warm and wet on my cheek.

Spit. Someone has spit on me.

Spit is not like sweat, not like urine. It is not clean.

It is not remotely sterile.

I am supposed to know how to do something other

than lie there, pretending to be asleep as my former best friend—I understand now, you are not my best friend, not anymore—scrambles away in the dark, retreating in giggles as the warm saliva runs down my cheek, toward my nose, tickling my skin as it goes.

taking over

THE NIGHT BEFORE MY SCIENCE REPORT, I couldn't turn my brain off.

I saw jellyfish when I closed my eyes.

Jellyfish when I opened them again and stared out into the blackness.

I got out of bed, turned on my light, and started pacing around the room, practicing what I was going to say.

I was muttering the report out loud when my door opened.

"Zu?" Mom asked. She wore a bathrobe and rubbed her eyes. "What are you doing?"

I shrugged.

"It's one thirty in the morning, Zu," she said. "Go to sleep."

But even when I lay down, I hovered at the line between sleep and waking.

In the morning, I was going to speak.

In the morning, I was going to tell everyone what I understood.

And when I was done—if all went as I hoped—I wouldn't be alone in my understanding anymore.

And if it didn't go as I'd hoped . . . well, then Jamie really would be the only one left.

how to not forget

THE ROCK LAKE CAMPOUT WAS DAYS AGO.
But I cannot get that frog out of my head.

I keep hearing it, the thud-splat of flesh against tree.
I remember its limbs flying outward as it sailed through
the air like a comic-strip image. But there was nothing
funny about it.

That frog had been helpless. Completely.

And your eyes looked right at me. The moment they
saw me, they changed.

You made a decision then, a decision not to care, a
decision about whose side you were on now.

And every time I think about that, I want to scream.

Shoot me if I ever become like that, *you said, long ago, when you swore you'd never be like Aubrey.*

Send me a signal, *you said.* A secret message. Make it big.

I tried. I tried to call your name and I choked on it.

I tried to tell you with my eyes. You looked away.

Thud. Splat.

It is almost the last day of school.

If I'm going to send you a message, I am running out of time.

part five

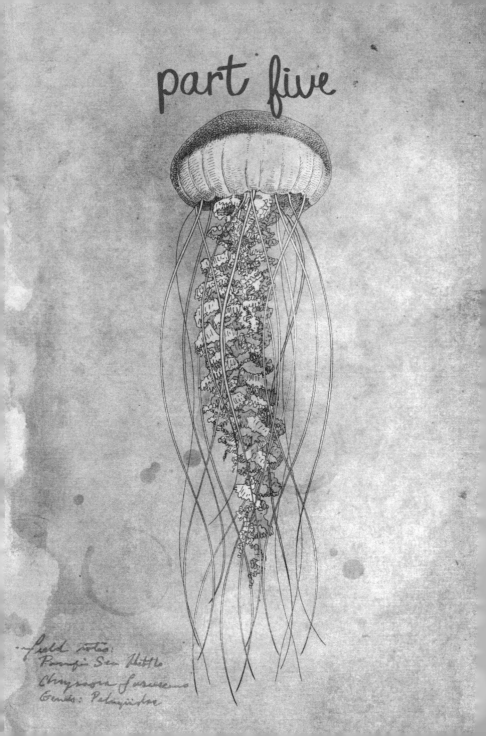

field notes:
Pacific Sea Nettle
Chrysaora fuscescens
Genus: Pelagiidae

Procedure

A well-written procedure section is fairly straightforward. What materials did you use? What did you do, and how did you do it?

—Mrs. Turton

stronger than us

Another thing you should know: Jellyfish are stronger than we are.

Consider this: A jellyfish sting is one of the fastest reactions in the animal kingdom. Their stingers are coiled like harpoons, millions of invisible weapons just waiting. When jellyfish tentacles brush a surface, even faintly, they spring into action. In just 700 billionths of a second—a tiny fraction of the time it would take a person to understand, to think, to react—the jellyfish releases those harpoons, all their poison, with the pressure of a bullet.

Jellies can sting long past their own death, long

after a tentacle is detached from the rest of the body. Jellyfish are stinging machines, and their stings are as violent as anything on Earth.

But they don't even have to think about that, about who they sting or why. Jellyfish don't get bogged down by drama, love, friendship, or sorrow. They don't get stuck in any of the stuff that gets people in trouble.

They connect with other members of their species only to mate, and even that happens without fuss. The male opens his mouth and releases sperm. The female passes through his sperm and accepts it. The whole affair is clean. Tidy. There is no touching or drama or passion or pain.

The parents never wonder about what happens next. They either reproduce or they do not. Their babies either survive or they do not. The babies don't think about the parents, and no jellyfish ever longs for another.

They drift past one another. They never stop moving, never stop pulsing through the depths.

imagine a creature

"Suzy?" Mrs. Turton smiled at me. "Are you ready?"

It was the day of my science report.

I walked to the front of my classroom with a stack of papers and several sheets of poster board. My heart pounded so hard I could hear it on the inside of my ears.

My feet moved across the tile floor. Fluorescent lights hummed overhead. Someone shifted in a chair, and the chair screeched. It was so loud I cringed.

I took a deep breath. I hadn't spoken to any of these kids since the last school year.

I wondered if I would even be able to speak out loud.

But I took that breath. And I closed my eyes. And I thought about Jamie.

I thought about the way he reached his hand into the swirl of tentacles, completely unafraid. About him writhing on a hospital bed in that red bathing suit, the way he let the whole world see him in the middle of his worst pain, when he felt like he was being shocked by a million electric needles.

If he could do *that*, surely I could do *this*.

I stared at the back wall. And then I spoke.

"Imagine a creature..." I started. Then I swallowed (my heart thumping so loudly).

"Imagine a creature so unlike other animals that scholars once believed it was a plant." (Deep breath.)

"A creature whose mouth and butt are one and the same." (Laughter then. Good. They were listening.)

"A creature that is dangerous to others even after it is dead."

I glanced around the room, just long enough to

notice Sarah Johnston leaning forward a little in her seat.

So I told them. I told them about jellyfish life cycles—that jellies start off almost like a plant, clinging to the bottom of the sea, and how in that phase of life, they are a *planula*. But when they are grown up, they break away from the seafloor and are free to pulse through the ocean. Then they have taken the form of a *medusa*.

I showed them a picture of a jellyfish that looks like a fried egg. I showed a picture of a jellyfish that looks like Darth Vader, and another that looks like a kindergartener's drawing of sunshine, just a big circle with lines sticking out in every direction. I showed them a jellyfish that lights up like police flashers when it's threatened, and another jellyfish that absorbs all the light that surrounds it.

"It's like a living black hole," I told my classmates, "a real live black hole inside the ocean."

I showed them picture after picture. And when I was done telling them all the basic things about jellyfish—what they eat and where they live and how they move and how many different forms they take—I began telling them other things.

The bad things.

I explained that jellyfish are taking over the seas.

That they are taking all the food for themselves.

That they are stealing penguins' food.

That they are driving the whales to extinction.

That many scientists believe that there are more jellyfish than ever before and that deadly jellyfish that used to be only in places like Australia are probably in other places now, too: in England. In Hawaii. In Florida. Maybe even closer.

Places like Maryland, even.

It was at that point that Mrs. Turton spoke. "I'm so sorry to interrupt, Suzy," she said gently. "But I'm afraid you're going to need to wrap up soon."

"I'm not finished," I said flatly.

"I love that you have so much to say," Mrs. Turton said. "But we still have another presentation to go, and we're running out of—"

"I'm *not finished*," I said. I said it louder and more forcefully than I'd ever spoken to a teacher. But I wasn't going to stop talking. Stopping now, at this moment, before I'd gotten to the most important things that needed to be explained, was impossible.

The class got very, very still then.

I stared at Mrs. Turton, and she lifted her eyebrows, surprised. Then she looked down at her lap, like she was thinking about something. When she looked up, she flashed a tight smile. "A few more minutes, Suzy," she said. "You can finish what you have to say, but please wrap up quickly."

I took a deep breath, and I got to the point. "The most frightening is probably the Irukandji. Deadly, transparent, and tiny—you won't even see this animal in the water."

I told them about the *number of documented deaths*. About the *migration over greater distances*. About the *dangerously fast heartbeat, brain hemorrhage*. About the *cause of deaths mistakenly attributed*.

And that's when I thought they would understand.

I really did: I thought everyone would understand.

"...And that is why we need to learn all we can about these fierce medusas of the sea," I said.

I stopped speaking. I swallowed. I took a deep breath.

Then I looked up.

Mrs. Turton watched me with that same look she'd had when I snapped at her. She was thinking hard about something, I could tell.

I think I did it, I thought, and I glanced around the room at my classmates to see if they, too, were thinking about what I'd said.

Some were looking at me, and some were not, and the ones who were looking at me didn't look like they were particularly moved.

One of the boys in the back of the room yawned.

Across from him, a girl carefully used her foot to push a folded piece of paper along the floor until it reached the desk of the girl in front of her. That girl dropped her pencil on the floor, then leaned down to pick up both the note and the pencil. She unfolded the note and let out a single snort of laughter.

Aubrey glanced at Molly with the same look she'd worn last year when I talked about the pee. Molly responded with a tiny gesture, so small that most people didn't see it. But I did; it was her moving her finger around in a circle next to her ear as if to say, *Crazy.*

Cray cray.

I glanced back at Mrs. Turton and understood then: She wasn't thinking about Franny. She *was* concerned, but her concern wasn't about how Franny died. Or jellyfish taking over the world.

It was about me.

Somehow, in this report, the most important words I'd ever spoken out loud, I'd done something wrong.

"Suzy," said Mrs. Turton finally, "that was *incredibly* thorough. I can see that a tremendous amount of hard work went into your presentation."

She turned to the rest of the class. "I'm afraid that puts us off our schedule, so I'm so sorry, Patrick, but you're going to have to go tomorrow." Patrick, a boy who is always doing his homework for the next class during whatever class he's already in, said "Yessss!" and pumped his fist like a motor.

And then everyone returned to normal, like I hadn't even spoken.

That's it? I wanted to say. I felt like saying *No, no, you didn't understand. Didn't you listen? Did you really listen?*

You don't understand that one of us might already have been taken by jellyfish?

And that maybe someday these animals will overtake us all?

I dropped some papers and looked straight at the floor as I gathered them. My hands were shaking.

Someone in the back of the room did that thing where you pretend to cough but you're really saying a word loud enough for everyone to hear.

The word was *Medusa.*

Everyone laughed. I turned around and saw Dylan looking at the ceiling, all innocent.

Then, when I turned back to the board, I heard it again, and this time I knew for sure that it was Dylan.

And then everyone started coughing like that.

"Medusa!"

I suddenly saw myself from the outside, as if I were watching from a corner of the classroom. I didn't see a girl who had just convinced the world of something important. Instead, I saw a weird, frizzy-haired girl with trembling hands and a blotchy red face. A girl with no friends. A girl whose face was screwing up in the ugliest way, tears starting to stream from her eyes.

Once the tears started, I was powerless to stop them.

"Medusa!"

"That's enough," said Mrs. Turton in a sharp voice.

The class quieted down, but I knew that from now on, my nickname would be Medusa.

"Go ahead and sit down, Suzy," said Mrs. Turton quietly. I nodded, and I rushed back to my seat.

I didn't want to just sit there and cry, not in front of all these kids. So as Mrs. Turton reviewed that night's homework, I opened my notebook and picked up my pen.

I wish I could meet you, Jamie. I wish I could meet you and you could tell me you understand. Because nobody else understands.

I tried, but they didn't see what I saw.

I know you would understand, because I have seen your picture. I found so many pictures of you online. In one, you're holding a jar, and inside that jar is an Irukandji, ghostly and transparent. Your eyes are soft as you look at it. In another, you are staring through a tank at a box jellyfish. The jellyfish is in the top of the tank, and you are beneath it, looking up. There are flecks in the water that look like stars in the night sky. And because your image is hazy through the glass, and you are on the other side of the water, you are the one who looks like a ghost.

And here is the thing that I find so interesting. There's never any anger in your eyes. There's never any disgust.

You don't even look at these creatures like they're all that different
from you.

You look curious, that's all—like you're
trying to figure them out. Like maybe
these creatures have something to tell
us, and you care enough to hear it.

What is it about you? How is it that
you care so much about the creatures
that everyone else hates? I mean, I
saw you in that hospital bed, almost
dead from a sting. Why aren't you the
least bit angry after that?

What is it about you that makes you
able to love creatures that no one else
can?

how to send a message

*U*RINE IS MORE THAN 95 PERCENT WATER. *That happens to be exactly the same way people describe jellyfish, by the way—more than 95 percent water—but this doesn't matter to me yet. Not yet. What matters now, as we near the end of sixth grade, is that freezing urine is easy.*

Send me a signal, *you had said. And for a long time, I didn't know how to do that. Then after the campout, after I felt that saliva on my cheek, I did.*

Make it big, *you'd said.*

Remember when I told you, that day in the cafeteria, that different animals use pee to communicate? That's what I've decided to do. I'm going to send a message delivered the same way you delivered your message: with body fluids.

I need thin, flat disks. These are easy to make, especially since I have been bringing home leftovers from Ming Palace every Saturday. Plastic takeout containers are perfect. The smallest size, the ones that are only a couple of inches high, are the best; these are easiest to stack neatly in the back of the freezer.

Peeing right into these containers is easy. I sit on the toilet and hold them underneath me, one at a time, stopping midstream to swap them out. I arrange the containers on the floor in front of me, then snap the lids on.

It's all very clean. Like I said once, on a day when none of my words came out quite right, urine is sterile. The only gross thing about it is that we think it's gross.

I was right about that, you know. I was right, even though those girls laughed, and you laughed, too.

After the lids are sealed tightly, I rinse the outsides, then place them in the freezer. I cover them with several packs of frozen vegetables, then place ice trays in front of the vegetables.

Then I go to bed. Tomorrow is the last day of sixth grade.

In the morning, as my mom showers, I stack the frozen plastic containers inside an insulated lunch pack, which I place in the bottom of my backpack. My stomach hurts, but I feel more sure than I have felt for a long time. I have even, at least for the moment, stopped hearing that terrible thud-splat inside my brain.

I tell Mom that my homeroom teacher invited kids to help clean out the classroom and ask her to drive me to school early. She doesn't ask any questions. Even when the parking lot is almost empty, she doesn't ask.

She trusts me, I think. Still trusts me, even if I no longer deserve it.

Maybe this is what happens when a person grows up. Maybe the space between you and the other people in your life grows so big you can stuff it full of all kinds of lies.

No one is in the hallway. Without any students, the hallway doesn't look like a real middle school; it looks like a movie set of a middle school. I imagine that it is the future, and that all the people have disappeared, and I am the only human left in the whole world. Outside, giant insects are roaming the planet; at any second they might appear at the double doors at the end of this hallway; they will come in and devour me, and that will be my end.

I feel the weight of the bag I'm carrying, my message for you, and I head toward the lockers.

terribly wrong

WHEN THE BELL RANG AFTER MY SCIENCE report was finished, Mrs. Turton said, "Suzy, hang back for a minute." I nodded but did not look up. I just kept staring at my desk as all the other kids gathered their books and walked out into the hallway, chattering as if my whole stupid report hadn't even happened.

As he passed my desk, Justin Maloney quietly placed a piece of notebook paper on my desk. The paper was covered with really messy sketches, each one of jellyfish, some of which looked like raggedy versions of the images I'd shown the class.

When the classroom was empty, Mrs. Turton said, "Suzy?"

I didn't say anything.

"Hey, Suzy," she said. She waited until I looked up. "That was a really good report. I can see how hard you worked. I rarely give As for these reports, but I'm giving you one. You deserve it."

I looked back down at Justin's sketches. They were sloppy but pretty accurate, actually.

"You know, Suzy," Mrs. Turton said, "I eat my lunches in here. You're welcome to join me. I'm always here if you want to talk."

Which reminded me of Dr. Legs, who was *the doctor I could talk to* but would rather not.

But the one I want to sit down with is Jamie. With Jamie I would know what to say.

"Or we could just sit and eat," Mrs. Turton said. "No talking necessary. Okay?"

I nodded, but I did not look at her. If I looked at her, I might start crying all over again.

"Be proud of yourself, Suzy," she said. "You did a terrific job today."

. I walked out of the class then, back into the hallway, thinking that this was another thing I didn't understand: how you can work so hard on a report, you can even earn an A, but you still walk away feeling like you've done something wrong.

Like you, yourself, are terribly wrong.

even more wrong

*W*HEN I REACH LOCKER NUMBER 605—
yours—I open the cooler. This is your message.
And you will understand.

The disks are frozen, but they have started to melt
around the edges. That's perfect; they slip out of the plastic
containers with ease.

Each locker has slats, which are angled upward. The
disks are exactly the right size to slip through the slats. I
work fast, but calmly, pressing each up through the slats of
your locker.

I ignore my stomach, which is cramping hard. I don't
know if any of this could have been different, if there was

some other message I could have sent, something I could have done sooner that would have allowed me to be sitting on the bus with you at this very moment, instead of here, slipping frozen pee disks into your locker.

I hear the clang when a frozen disk hits the back of the locker, the hushed thud when one lands on something soft.

It wasn't that long ago that I slipped notes into your locker, marked with BFF *and* FOR YOUR EYES ONLY *and our nicknames—*MIZZ FRIZZ *and* STRAWBERRY GIRL. *This is a different kind of note.*

You shouldn't have laughed at me. You shouldn't have called me weird. You shouldn't have spit on me.

But I want you to know: This isn't about revenge. This is me doing the very thing you asked me to do. It's me trying to make you listen. To finally, really listen. It's about trying to save us before you disappear completely.

You will be shocked at first. You will look up, right at me, as if to say, What have you done?

And I will stare at you. Hard. And with my eyes, I will tell you, You told me to do something big.

Then it will dawn on you: I did something big, because I had to.

I did something big, because you told me to.

I did something big, because it was time. It was time to bring you back. To bring us back.

And that's when the look on your face will change, and your eyes will say, Did I really hurt you that much?

And my eyes will tell you, Yes.

And your eyes will say, I understand.

And then your eyes will say, I'm sorry.

And then we'll be even. We'll be able to start again.

I imagine the disks hitting your pink Red Sox sweatshirt, falling past the decorations that hang on the inside of your locker door—the cutout magazine images of cats, the polka-dot magnetic mirror, the photos of your new friends, the ones that one day replaced the picture of the two of us standing together at Six Flags. When I think of your new photos, I push the disks especially hard.

As soon as the last one is gone, I snatch the empty plastic containers and lids, and I stuff them back into the insulated cooler. I take the lunch pack to the girls' bathroom and stuff it in the garbage bin, covering it with crumpled paper towels.

Then I walk to the sink to wash my hands.

And it's while I'm standing there, in front of the mirror, that I feel something else. The back of my neck throbs. One of my eyelids spasms. I grip the sink and try to look in the mirror, but everything is blurry. Whatever this feeling is, I want to run from it, but my legs don't want to hold me up. I sink down onto the floor.

In forty minutes, the hallways will fill with kids. The ice will have melted. Your locker will be soaked.

venom

The thing you and I understand, Jamie, is that having venom doesn't make a creature bad. Venom is protection.

The more fragile the animal, the more it needs to protect itself. So the more venom a creature has, the more we should be able to forgive that animal. They're the ones that need it most.

And, really, what is more fragile than a jellyfish, which doesn't even have any bones?

I think you understand this. I just wanted you to know that I do, too.

I wish we could sit down and talk about these things. About stings and venoms and beginnings and endings and all the creatures that no one else seems to understand.

look at me

I AM STANDING AT MY LOCKER WHEN *I* SEE YOU *approach. My heart beats more steadily now. The cold, sticky, sweaty feeling has stopped. Only that churning in my stomach remains.*

Just before you arrive at your locker, I close my own and walk toward homeroom. I count the seconds. I don't look back at you, not yet, but I know anyway: Now you are turning the dial of your combination lock. Now you are lifting the handle of the locker. Now you are reaching in.

When I hear the commotion, I do not turn around.

Someone shouts, "Gross!" Then, from other kids, I hear "Ew!" and "Piss! It's piss!"

"*Oh, man, somebody took a leak in her locker!*"

I hear laughter. I hear the footsteps of kids running over to see what's happening. I feel the commotion, feel the energy out there, like it has a shape, volume, weight. It is something I could reach out and touch if I were to turn around.

I focus on the air going in and out of my lungs.

Somebody says, "I'll go tell the main office." I hear footsteps running.

I stand in the doorway of homeroom. I adjust my books slowly, carefully.

I look up only when the crowd moves away.

Your shoulders are rounded, like you have crumpled into yourself. Crying, *I think, feeling strangely disconnected from my own thoughts.* Franny is crying.

Now you need to look at me. For the message to work, for you to understand, you have *to look at me.*

The bell rings. Kids filter past me into the classroom. They're still laughing.

The homeroom teacher tells everyone to sit down, but I linger in the doorway.

Look at me, *I think.*

The teacher says, "Suzanne Swanson, please join us."

There is a pencil sharpener near the door. I dig in my bag, pull out a pencil, and place it in the sharpener. I turn the handle very slowly.

Mrs. Hall, the school secretary, approaches you with plastic bags. You fill the plastic bags with your belongings, one at a time. Your shoulders are shaking hard now.

The homeroom teacher asks the kids to begin emptying their desks. I continue to turn the pencil sharpener.

Look. At. Me.

And then you and Mrs. Hall walk toward the office. She does not offer to carry any of the bags. You get farther away with each step. If you don't turn around soon, you won't even be able to see my eyes.

Together, you round a corner.

Then you disappear.

I do not wonder if this is the last image I will ever have of you on this Earth. Why would I wonder such a thing?

What I am thinking now is simply this: You did not look.

It's not a new beginning to you, I realize. It is something else entirely.

It's some sort of ending.

I place one hand on the wall to steady myself, and I turn back to the classroom, where kids are pulling heaps of paper out of their desks. The homeroom teacher is saying that if everyone gets things cleaned up quickly, we can have a paper airplane contest with some of these papers. Everyone cheers. Everyone but me.

I feel nothing at all.

The nothing stays with me for the rest of these final, useless hours of sixth grade—as kids toss paper airplanes around the room, as I sit alone through the end-of-the-year picnic, as the buses pull out of the parking lot, this terrible school year fading away.

It's only later that I feel something.

It's only later, when I step into the bathroom and sit down on the toilet and find a single red spot of blood in my underpants. The blood is a surprise. When I see it, I feel a deep wave of shame. It blares its crimson color at me like a warning.

Or maybe an accusation.

pollination

AFTER MY SCIENCE REPORT, KIDS STARTED coughing "Medusa" into their hands every time I passed in the hallway.

They did it for the rest of that day, and then—just to make sure it wasn't a one-day thing—when I returned to school again in the morning.

That was just one of the reasons I decided to visit Mrs. Turton at lunchtime.

I stood in the doorway and cleared my throat.

"Oh," she said, brightening a little. "Suzy. Come on in."

She brought a second chair over to her desk and patted it. "How are you doing?" she asked as I sat.

I looked at her shoes. They were brown leather boots, well worn, with fringe coming down in the back. They looked at once practical and adventurous—the kind of boots that could really take a person somewhere. I imagined the hallways outside this room as a desert filled with enemies in khaki, Mrs. Turton dashing through the harsh landscape in an effort to save the world.

"Suzy, you're a terrific student," she said, "but I'm concerned about you. I talked with some of your teachers from last year, and it sounds like there have been some changes in your behavior this year. Change is normal. Everybody changes. But I wanted to make sure you're okay. Are you?"

I kept my eyes on her boots. I nodded.

"Good," she said, sounding like she wasn't all that convinced. "That's good to know."

There was a long pause, and then she changed the subject. "You seem to really like science. Am I right?"

I thought about that. I liked a lot of the things she showed us, and a lot of the things I found online.

I liked the way patterns repeated themselves in this universe, the way a solar system could resemble an atom, or a mountain range seen from outer space could look just like a fern leaf covered with frost. I liked the thought that three billion bugs fly over my head in a single month in summer or that an inch of soil might contain millions of creatures from thousands of different species.

These things made me feel like I could stand in one place my whole life and never run out of new things to discover. I liked that so many things were out there, waiting to be known.

But sometimes studying science uncovered other, scarier things. I didn't like thinking about predators and prey, about a rabbit thrashing in a fox's jaws. I didn't like lying in bed knowing that even if we could figure out how to travel at the speed of light, which no one can, we wouldn't get to the edge of the universe for 46 billion years, which is triple the amount of time anything has even existed. And worse, the universe is expanding so fast that by the time you got to the edge of today's universe, the universe would have grown so much bigger that you could never, ever get to the edge.

No matter how hard we tried, we'd be stuck in an in-between place—nowhere, really—forever.

I didn't like being on a pale blue dot, surrounded by nothing, a nothing that expanded around us in every direction.

"I'd like to show you something, Suzy," Mrs. Turton said.

She typed into her computer, tilted the monitor toward me, and pulled up a video.

"I just watched this last night. Perhaps you'll like it."

She pressed Play, then picked up some papers and started grading. I liked that she left me alone like that.

At first, the video showed just a man talking on a stage in front of a bunch of people. The man had a little lisp and he was describing pollination, which he described as *nature's way to reproduce.*

Then, on the screen in front of me, there was a time-lapse image of a flower unfolding. The flower had these delicate outside petals, which opened to reveal long spikes with violet stripes.

This is one of the good kinds of blooms, I thought. *The word* bloom *can have so many meanings. Jellyfish blooms might be terrifying. But some blooms—like this one—can be beautiful.*

Someone appeared in Mrs. Turton's doorway. Justin Maloney.

"Mrs. Turton?" he said. He glanced at me. "Oh, hey, Belle."

I was so busy watching the video in front of me that I didn't even bother to make a face at him for calling me the wrong name.

Mrs. Turton looked up from her desk. "Ah, Mr. Maloney. Have you completed your bibliography?"

"Yeah," he said, sort of sheepishly. He handed her a paper.

She examined it, then nodded. "Thank you. I'll add it to your report. But next time, I expect it *with* your report. It's an essential part, okay?"

He nodded and turned to leave. Then he asked, "Whatcha watching, Belle?"

"Shhh," I hissed at him. That name again. Belle. I kept my eyes on the computer screen.

A bee lifted off a flower in slow motion, like an airplane rising. It joined a group of bees, whose wings beat together like a million heartbeats.

"Whoa," said Justin.

"Pull up a chair, if you want," said Mrs. Turton. I frowned. But Justin either didn't notice or didn't care. He pulled a chair over.

As he sat, the screen showed bats flying through the desert at night. Their skeletons were visible through their wings in the moonlight.

Justin whistled, then asked, "Seriously, what is this?"

I didn't know. It seemed to me it was about everything beautiful.

Then, in front of us on the screen, there were a million monarch butterflies, dancing in slow motion in the sky. All that fluttering, that color, yellow against blue, the in-and-out movement of their wings. I thought something inside me might crack in two.

When it was done, Justin said, "Hey, can we go back to the part with the bats?"

So we did.

"I wish the world looked like that all the time," murmured Justin.

Mrs. Turton looked up from her paperwork. "It does," she said.

We watched the video again and again, until the bell rang and lunch was over and it was time for math class.

As we stepped into the hall, Justin said, "Thanks for letting me watch with you, Belle. That was cool."

That was the third time he'd called me that. *Belle.* I didn't know why he was calling me names, or why he'd chosen that particular one. But I'd had enough.

I stopped and put my hands on my hips.

"That's their biggest part, right?" he asked. "A bell?"

I stared at Justin. He shifted his backpack from one shoulder to the other, and his mouth curled into the tiniest half-smile.

I realized he was talking about jellyfish. The bell

is the round part of the jellyfish that pulses like a heart—it's the only part you can touch without getting stung.

"I've never been a fan of Medusa," he said. "All those creepy snakes in her hair." He fake-shuddered. "But Belle is an okay name, don't you think?"

Justin isn't going to call me Medusa, I thought. *He's telling me this.* For a kid who had recently gotten detention for throwing paperback dictionaries out our English classroom window, he was maybe not so bad.

We walked the rest of the way to math class in silence, but it was the best kind of silence. It was the *not-talking* kind of silence, the kind that so few people seemed to understand.

the worst kind of silence

*A*FTER THE FAILED MESSAGE I TRIED TO SEND
*you, the one that got your stuff drenched in pee, I
wait for the phone to ring. It's going to ring, and it's not
going to be good.*

*I don't know who will be calling. Maybe it will be the
principal, maybe it will be Mrs. Hall who did not hold
your bags. Maybe it will be your mom.*

*Your mom. Who would have washed those wet clothes
and held you as you cried.*

*Maybe it won't be a phone call at all. Maybe it will be
like on television, where they send police to the house and
lead me out of there in handcuffs.*

There is nothing to do but wait.

When my mom walks in and asks, "Do you want to go out to dinner? Celebrate the end of the school year?" I think, Mom, you are going to be so mad at me.

I will try to explain. I will try to help her understand, but I already know she won't. If you didn't understand, and you're the one who asked for a secret message in the first place, then why would anyone else?

Even I don't understand anymore.

two days' silence

A DAY OF SILENCE IS TOO LONG. BUT TWO DAYS *of silence is unbearable.*

They are probably gathering evidence, I tell myself.

I mean, you must know it was me. You might not have understood what I meant, but somehow I'm sure you know I did it.

So where is everyone?

The phone doesn't ring, the doorbell doesn't ring, and my mother keeps smiling at me as if all is okay and every-thing is normal.

It would be so much better if we could just get it over with.

and then more silence

*I*T IS ONLY *AFTER FOUR DAYS PASS THAT I BEGIN* *to imagine other possibilities.*

Maybe you are waiting to talk to me.

Maybe you are planning your own message.

Or maybe you know, above all, that your silence is the worst, hardest thing of all.

That's when I begin to understand that the phone isn't going to ring. Nobody will come to our doorstep. Not today or tomorrow, not the day after that.

I don't know what I will say the next time I see you.

The thing I did hangs suspended between us. It hovers there, silently, like an unfinished sentence.

what i don't want to talk about

*I*DON'T WANT TO TALK ABOUT WHAT HAPPENED
at St. Mary Magdalene Episcopal Church, South
*Grove, Massachusetts, sixty-seven days after the end
of sixth grade, just four days before the start of seventh
grade.*

*I don't want to talk about how sticky hot it was, and
how crowded, and how my mom and I got there early
but there were already so many people we couldn't get
a seat. I don't want to remember how it felt to stand in
the entryway of the church, trying hard to breathe even
though the air felt like soup and everyone was standing
too close.*

I hissed at my mom, "Who are all these people?" and she whispered back, "Funerals are different when it's a child." I would have pointed out that she hadn't exactly answered my question, but then I noticed how grim her mouth was, the way all those tight lines radiated out from the edges of her lips.

So I don't want to talk about that, just like I don't want to talk about that droning organ that played so slowly and sadly that it took me almost the whole song to realize it was playing "Somewhere Over the Rainbow." Or how I looked down at the program in my hands (Where did it come from? Who had handed it to me, and when?) and looked at that photograph of you. You were standing at the beach, squinting out at the water with your bathing suit strap digging into your freckled shoulder.

(You had a new pageboy haircut, and I thought, Cute. But then I realized that cute had been your word, and my stomach turned a little.)

The caption beneath your picture said: LAST PHOTO. TAKEN AUGUST 19. Which by then we all knew was the day you died.

It seemed unbelievably cruel to put that photo on the cover of your program for everyone to see.

I recognized some people, like the guidance counselors from school, and Mrs. Turton, who hadn't even had you in a class yet and now never would. I saw your next-door neighbor, the lady whose husband died before we were born and who sometimes let us swim in her pool. I was surprised to see my own father, almost unrecognizable in a dark suit, standing near Aaron and Rocco. I saw the school principal, and your great-aunt Lynda, who we called Shelf Butt, because her butt was so big a person could set a glass of milk on it.

And closer to me, I saw two girls sitting in one of the last pews, their backs rounded, their hair pulled back into perfect ponytails. Aubrey and Molly. Their shoulders were shaking, and I could tell they were crying.

Here is something you might not know: that sometimes, at a funeral, what a person feels is hatred. I'm telling you, I hated those girls then—hated that they had a pew, that they didn't have to feel frizzy hair tickling the backs of their necks. I hated that they were there at all. But most of all, I hated that they were crying, hated that they felt close enough to you that they would cry, when all I could do was stand there, stiff and sick to my stomach. It was like their tears, or my lack of them, were proof: proof that you'd been right when you left me, that I'd never deserved you after all.

No, I don't want to talk about any of that stuff. Not now, not ever.

But I will tell you three things.

First: That church fluttered. Everyone there was trying so hard to be still, to sit straight. But the thing is, they couldn't. They waved their programs like fans. They dabbed their eyes. Their backs rose and fell and rose and fell and sometimes shook. The whole place filled with rustling and sniffles and sighs and cries, so much movement it was almost dizzying. Except, I realized, one box at the front of the church, which was so utterly motionless.

And you were inside that box: perfect and still and twelve years old, forever and ever.

Second: Two birds danced near the rafters. I swear, I was the only person in that church who saw them. Everyone else looked forward, they looked down, they leaned against one another. But if they'd only looked up, they would have seen the sweeping dips and flutters of the dark birds.

Last: After it was over—after the men wheeled your box away and your mom stumbled after it with wild eyes, and after I stood outside and watched all those strangers/not-strangers file out of the building, the only thing I wanted to do was scream. And what I wanted to scream was this: I hate you. I hate all of you. *I didn't just hate the other kids for being sad, for believing that the sorrow belonged to them, somehow, when you were never theirs to begin with. I also hated the adults, for not trying to fix this situation, for not making it better somehow. I hated them all for just giving up.*

That was the thing. Everyone else had just given up.

But I hadn't. Not when I hugged my father hello and goodbye, and not when Rocco and Aaron came up to me and Aaron hugged me for a long, long time, and not when my mom and I walked silently to her car. Not when I saw the dashboard with the dust on it and the mirror with the warning about how objects are closer than they appear.

Everything was supposedly over and we were sup-posed to start getting on with life.

But I was sure: I wasn't going to accept this thing that had happened, the way all those others were doing.

things are closer than they appear

"Zu." I heard Mom's voice as if it came from another land entirely. Then her hand was on my shoulder, and for just a moment, she was inexplicably next to me as I moved through the water.

Then I opened my eyes and looked around.

My room.

Dreaming. I'd been dreaming. Jamie had been there.

"Zu, what are you still doing in bed? I woke you up forty minutes ago!"

I blinked. Mom was in her work clothes, but her hair was disheveled.

Mom threw back the covers; I curled into a ball.

I didn't want to do anything but fall backward into the dream I'd been having.

"Come on, Zu," Mom insisted. "You knew I didn't have time to drive you to school today. I thought you were getting ready all this time."

I groaned and sat up.

"*Hair. Teeth. Hurry,*" she said.

As I got ready, I tried to remember everything I could about the dream.

I had been in the water when Mom woke me. I was looking at Jamie's laboratory. His lab was stark white, and it sat on the water—not a building at the edge of the water, like the aquarium. Instead, it floated right on top of the water, surrounded on all sides by clear blue sea.

I had to swim to get to Jamie. He smiled at me as if he knew me and understood why I was there. It was like he was saying, *Are you coming or not?*

The water around Jamie's lab, I knew, was filled with Irukandji. I don't know how I knew that, but I did.

But I'd lowered myself into the water and started swimming toward him anyway.

As I got close, Jamie held out his hand. That's when I saw an Irukandji, just millimeters from my skin.

I was about to reach out for Jamie, and I was about to get stung. Both, at the same time. I didn't know which would happen first.

I was on the verge of understanding something in that moment. Something important.

I heard a drawer thrown open in the kitchen and the clink of silverware. "Come on, Zu!" Mom called from the kitchen.

It was hard to think with her making all that noise. *What was so important about that dream?*

When I got to the kitchen, Mom was smearing butter on toast. "You're going to have to eat this on the bus," she said. I noticed she was wearing two entirely different shoes.

I pointed to her feet. It took her a moment to register what I was telling her, and then she grumbled, "Oh, for heaven's sake." She thrust the toast at me. "Here," she said as she glanced at the clock and ran back to her bedroom. I could hear her rummaging in her closet until she emerged, holding a different pair of shoes. "You've got your books?"

I nodded.

Mom rushed me out the door, following right behind me. She ran to the car in bare feet, still holding her shoes. As she backed out of the driveway, she rolled down the window. "Have a good day," she called. The school bus lumbered toward me.

I hated that I had to go to school. I hated being stuck here—in seventh grade, in South Grove, in this place of never being able to undo anything.

And that's when I understood:

Whatever was about to happen next in that dream—whether I reached Jamie or got stung—it was better than staying still. The staying still was the worst part. The waiting and not-knowing and being afraid: That was worse than anything else that might happen.

Worse, even, than getting stung.

Maybe it's not so crazy, I realized. *Maybe I should go see Jamie.*

I mean, why not, really?

bridget brown

ONE SUMMER, A COUPLE OF YEARS AGO, THREE children stepped on a plane in Jacksonville, Florida. They flew all the way to Nashville, Tennessee. They were not with any adults.

It was all over the news when it happened. I saw it on *Good Morning America*. Bridget Brown, a fifteen-year-old, had saved $700 from babysitting. She asked her brother, Cody, who was eleven, and their thirteen-year-old neighbor, Bobby, where they wanted to go. Bobby suggested Nashville. He wanted to go to see Dollywood, which is a big theme park with roller coasters and a steam engine.

Bridget Brown and Cody and Bobby took a cab to the airport. They bought tickets at the counter and got all the way to Nashville, which is 501 miles from Jacksonville, which is 2,645,280 feet and 32 million inches. Nobody asked them for identification. Nobody stopped them.

In fact, the man who handed them their tickets told them they'd better rush so that they didn't miss their flight.

If the kids had done their research—if they'd done any planning whatsoever—they would have known to fly to Knoxville instead of Nashville. That's because Dollywood is only 38 miles from Knoxville, but it is a full 200 miles from Nashville.

Once their plane landed, they didn't have enough money to get to the park.

I imagine them standing in the airport, counting their money and trying not to draw any attention to themselves. I wonder how long they stayed in the airport trying to figure out what to do.

Eventually, they called their parents and flew home.

Here was the problem with fifteen-year-old Bridget

Brown: She didn't know how to plan. If she'd looked at a map, counted her money, researched average cab fares and highways and traffic conditions, those kids would have made it.

They would have gotten all the way to Dollywood.

There are other documented cases of kids flying by themselves—plenty of cases like this one. But here is the thing I remembered about Bridget Brown's story: She didn't break any rules. What she did was perfectly legal.

Kids over twelve are allowed to fly alone.

I looked it up to be sure, and it's true. Read any article about Bridget Brown. There's always a sentence that says something like this: *Airline policy clearly states passengers age twelve and over may travel with no adult supervision as long as they have a valid boarding pass.*

Which means you can go anywhere. You just need a good plan, a destination, money to get you there, and enough deep breaths that you don't lose your nerve.

You can just step onto the plane and disappear.

deadline

THAT DAY IN SCHOOL, SIGNS BEGAN APPEARING in the hallway.

Winter Dance

FEBRUARY 10

VOTE FOR YOUR FAVORITE THEME

THEMES INCLUDE:

MIDNIGHT IN PARIS • *TROPICAL PARADISE* • *HEROES AND VILLAINS* • *AN EVENING IN HOLLYWOOD*

YOU MAY VOTE IN THE MAIN OFFICE.
ONE VOTE PER STUDENT

Ugh, I thought. A school dance.

I could just imagine what my mom would say if she knew about the dance.

Go, she'd say. *You should go, it might be fun.*

I looked at the sign again and saw the date: February 10. It wasn't that far away.

And that's when I made up my mind about three things:

1. I wasn't going to vote on a theme.
2. I wasn't going to attend the dance.
3. I would be out of the country by
   February 10.

That's when I knew for sure. I was really going to do it. I was going to get myself to Australia.

And I had a deadline.

instant calm

IT WAS FUNNY HOW MUCH BETTER I FELT AS SOON as I made the decision to go to Australia. It was like an instant calm, a sudden relief, came over me. Nothing had changed, and yet everything had.

I had a plan. I was leaving.

It felt like someone had opened a crack in the door, allowing a single beam of light to stream through. Just knowing there was light on the other side made it easier to be around all those kids who called me Medusa and talked about school dances.

All I had to do was get my things in order— get the money I needed, buy a ticket, get to Jamie.

Then everything would be different. I would be understood.

CʒⓏ ⓈƆ

I continued to have lunch in Mrs. Turton's room every day. Justin often joined me. "Better here than in the lunchroom," he said once, the only explanation he ever gave for being there.

Mrs. Turton never seemed to mind that Justin spilled cookie crumbs all over the floor, or that I rarely responded to anyone with more than a shrug. If Justin called me Belle, she never stopped to ask why; she let us be.

It was like she trusted us. Trusted that if she gave us this space, we'd be okay.

She often had something interesting to show us. For example, she might bring out a book she thought we might enjoy looking at—a collection of photographs from the deep sea, or one filled with images from a microscope so powerful that a single human hair looked like a sequoia rising from the earth.

One day, she showed us a video in which a scientist described what he called "the most astounding fact," which was that all living things are composed of the atoms of collapsed stars. The stars themselves were inside us.

We were made of stardust.

And that reminded me of what Mrs. Turton had told us about how we were all walking around with bits of Shakespeare inside us.

Sarah Johnston knocked on the door. "Mrs. Hall asked me to bring this to you," she said, handing Mrs. Turton a piece of paper. Then she noticed me and Justin.

"Sorry," she whispered to us.

Mrs. Turton took the paper. "Thanks, Sarah." She smiled.

Sarah turned to leave, then paused in the doorway. *Yes*, the astronomer was saying. *Yes, we are a part of this universe, we are in this universe, but perhaps more important than both of those facts is that the universe is in us.*

Sarah lingered in the doorway, watching the

computer over our shoulders. Mrs. Turton said to her, "Take a seat, Sarah. Join us."

Sarah glanced at me and Justin, and I had the feeling that she wanted to stay.

I frowned. Sarah must have noticed.

"Um, I don't think so," she said. She ducked out.

Good, I thought. *The last thing I need is another person cluttering up my life right now.* Especially when I was about to leave it.

how to plan your escape

WHEN YOU ARE TRAVELING TO CAIRNS, Australia, at the edge of the Great Barrier Reef, to answer a question that no one else has asked, you need quite a bit of money.

The ticket would cost over a thousand dollars, even one way. I needed a credit card to buy it.

I didn't have a credit card. But both of my parents did. And as it happened, my dad paid for our Ming Palace dinners every Saturday night with a bright blue credit card.

It happened the same way every week. There was kind of a rhythm to these nights: the fried noodles, drinks, soup. The sound of food sizzling and the neon sign flickering in the window, CHINESE FOOD, OPEN. Then later, after dinner, the way the server set down the bill. Then Dad placed his credit card on the table before getting up to wash the moo shu off his hands.

Every Ming Palace dinner unfolded like this, every time. It was almost like waves lapping at a shore. A person could notice, or not.

I noticed.

After a few weeks of paying attention, I picked up the credit card when Dad left the table. I held it and counted the seconds before the server came to take the card.

One, two, three, four . . . all the way up to forty-one.

I tried it again for the next couple of weeks. Sometimes I had an even longer time alone with the card—91 seconds, 83 seconds, 123 seconds.

One night in December, I brought a pink index

card to dinner with me. When Dad left the table, I began writing down what I saw on the card.

The following week, I brought the index card with me again.

It took four different dinners—all the way into the new year—to get all the information down. I copied the whole thing, every number and letter from his credit card. I wrote down the words that were in the upper left corner of his card: *Chase* and *Freedom*. I thought that was maybe what my English teacher would call an oxymoron, because you cannot truly have freedom if someone is chasing you.

On the other hand, maybe it was not an oxymoron. Maybe what I was doing was, in fact, chasing some sort of freedom.

I copied all of it: the four trapezoids that came together in a kind of circle, which was the logo of the Chase Freedom credit card. The good-through date and the exact way his name appeared on the card: JAMES P SWANSON.

I wrote down everything on the back side, too, including the things that didn't seem important. The statement that *use of this card is subject to the card member agreement*, the twenty-four-hour customer service number. I even drew the shiny eagle that appeared and disappeared depending on which way I held the card. I left nothing out.

The index card was always back in my pocket by the time Dad returned to the table.

But by January, I had it all. My pink index card was an accurate replica of my dad's shiny blue plastic card.

When I went home that night, I tucked the index card into the back of my sock drawer.

I did not wonder whether I was doing the right thing or the wrong thing. My dad would understand later. After I had proved what needed to be proved—after I'd had the chance to explain it—he would understand.

spare change

THERE WAS ANOTHER THING I NEEDED TO
travel to Queensland, Australia, at the edge
of the Great Barrier Reef.

I needed cash. My dad's credit card would not be
enough. I needed cash for cab fare, for food. And
I thought it might be best to pay for my hotel with
cash, too. That would make it a little harder for my
parents to find me.

I didn't want anyone to find me until I'd gotten
the answer I needed.

There were a few ways to get cash. First, I smashed

my piggy bank. For years, I'd been dropping money in there—spare change I'd picked up around the house, or my $5-per-week allowance that I got when Mom remembered to give it to me or I remembered to ask.

Other kids spend their money at the mall, or seeing movies with friends. But I don't like the mall, and I didn't have any friends to go to the movies with.

I counted out each $5 bill, each crumpled dollar, each coin. I was surprised to discover that I already had $283.62 saved. That was a lot of money, but it wasn't enough.

I needed more, so I turned to my mom.

Each week, I took a little money out of my mom's wallet. Never too much: If she had forty dollars in her wallet, I might take four or five of those dollars. If she had twenty-one dollars, I took three or four. A different mother might keep track of her dollars more closely, but not mine. My mom was so scattered, just barely getting to her house showings on time, always rummaging around in cabinets and closets for something she couldn't find.

Mom never kept track of anything too closely.

She still gave me money for milk and a snack in the cafeteria every day, even though I now spent every lunch period in Mrs. Turton's room.

Adding it all together—the lunch money, the taken-from-her-wallet money, the loose bills and change—might give me another $250 or so, depending on when I left.

Altogether, I hoped to gather $500 in cash. That way, I'd have enough for taxi fares, a bunch of meals, and maybe a few nights' stay in a not-very-nice hotel.

It was hard to know what would happen after that. I was assuming that my parents would help me out once they found out where I was. But I wasn't sure. Maybe they would be so angry that they would decide to just leave me there, make me find my own way home. I really couldn't imagine what they'd do.

The truth is, anytime I thought that far ahead, I didn't want to think about it anymore.

I placed the cash in a big envelope, and I watched the envelope grow.

Taking the money from Mom's purse felt so bad sometimes that my stomach hurt and I had to lie down. I told myself I was doing the right thing. After all, Mom was the one who'd told me *Sometimes things just happen*. She was the one who hadn't understood in the first place.

Maybe if she could have shown me that the world still made sense in some way, that there was still some sort of order to things—I might not even be doing this.

But she hadn't. She'd shrugged her shoulders and said, *Sometimes things just happen*, and expected somehow that this would be enough.

So I didn't exactly have a choice about taking her money.

I did not want to be like fifteen-year-old Bridget Brown.

I wanted to be prepared.

goodbye, thor

O N THE DAY OF THE EARTHWORM DISSEC-
tion, Justin and I sat in the science lab, staring down at the tray in front of us. There were some
knives for slicing, and a bunch of pins with colorful
plastic heads. There was a magnifying glass, plus a
little bowl of sterilizing fluid.

In the middle of the tools, a dead worm just sat in
a Pyrex cup.

I stared at it. Justin watched me.

"You're going to need me to do the slicing and
dicing, aren't you?" Justin asked.

I nodded.

"Don't worry, Belle," he said. He patted my arm. "I got this one."

He picked up the dead earthworm with tweezers and laid it out on the table in front of us. It looked just like every other earthworm I'd ever seen, except that it lay there like a limp piece of string.

It reminded me of Angel Yanagihara's mouse. And of that frog that Dylan threw against the tree last year. The smell of preservatives filled my nose.

Justin picked up a knife. He poked the worm gently.

Then he hesitated.

"You know what? I think we should give this guy a name," he said. "He should have some dignity."

I liked that idea. I smiled.

"How 'bout Moe?" he said. I made a face. "Evil Peter the Soil Eater?" I shook my head. "Thor?"

Thor. A big name for such a little guy. I smiled, just a tiny bit. But it was enough.

"O mighty Thor," Justin said, looking down at

the worm. "You may be small in size, but your leg-less little life is a great gift to our understanding of the scientific method. And also our ability to pass seventh grade."

Justin kept right on talking as he made a clean slice down the middle of the earthworm. "Hey, speaking of names, isn't Belle the real name of Snow White?"

"Beauty," I said.

He looked up, surprised. Then he grinned from ear to ear.

I'm not sure what made me decide to speak to Justin. Maybe it was the fact that he didn't need me to, that he was perfectly content to keep up the conversation all by himself. Maybe it was because I didn't have anything to lose anymore—in a few days, I'd be gone.

"Well, well, well," he said. "She *does* talk."

"I can talk. When there's something to say. And it was Beauty."

"Beauty?"

"And the Beast. Her name was Belle."

"Oh." He thought for a moment. "So does that make me the Beast?"

I shrugged.

"The Beast was a bad guy, right?" he asked.

I shook my head. "He was okay. He just scared people who didn't know him, that's all."

"Huh," said Justin. "That sounds about right."

Justin carefully peeled back the sides of the earthworm to reveal the gray gizzard, the glistening reproductive parts, like miniature white beans fresh from the can. I took notes as he moved the parts of the worm around.

Right in the middle of the dissection, Justin's stopwatch went off and he had to put down the scalpel. He reached into his pocket and pulled out his pill.

I held out my hand, palm open.

He hesitated. "Um, I don't think you should take that, Belle," he said.

I made a face at him—of course I wasn't going to take his stupid medicine   and he handed it to me.

I turned the pill over. On one side, there was a hexagon with a line coming off one end. It looked like a six or a nine, or maybe a geometric snail. I handed the pill back.

"What's the difference?" I asked.

"The difference?"

"Before you take it and after."

"Ah." He furrowed his brow. "Well...before I take it," he started slowly, "it's like everything comes in at once, so fast I can't quite grab on to any of it."

"What things?"

"All of it. Everything." He looked around the room. "Like, the clock ticking, and the colors of kids' clothes and the lists I make in my head and all the talking and the homework I forgot to do and the hard seat and the fact that next we are going to PE and maybe we'll play volleyball but maybe we'll play that freeze-dance game, and the fact that my arm itches and there's sleet falling, and all of it. It's all just kind of jumbled together. And it's loud, too. All those thoughts are so loud I can't quite make sense of any of them. But then I take my medicine, and even though I don't *feel* any different, it's like the world around me has changed."

He bit his lip and tried to explain more. "Everything just gets less...confusing. Like there's space between all those things. It's less noisy, somehow."

He shook his head. "I don't know. It's really hard to describe."

Then he looked at the pill in his hand. "Bottoms up," he said. He tossed it into his mouth and swallowed.

"Like an orchestra," I said quietly.

"Huh?"

"Like the difference between hearing random noises versus hearing an orchestra," I said.

"Yeah," he said, like he was thinking out loud. I could hear that he was surprised. "Yeah, that's exactly right."

When I looked up, he was looking at me, kind of admiring. That made me uncomfortable, so I just said, "We should finish this."

And actually, finishing the dissection wasn't too bad. It was more interesting than horrible.

Before the class was over, Justin spoke to Thor one more time.

"Thank you, mighty Thor," he said, "for showing us your seminal receptacles. May you rest in peace now."

how to say goodbye

IN EARLY FEBRUARY, JUST A WEEK BEFORE THE dance, I sat with Dr. Legs again.

"Anything you feel like talking about today, Suzanne?"

I shook my head.

We sat in silence for a long while. In my head, I reviewed the lists of all the things I would need on my trip.

I had almost everything at this point: an envelope of money, phone numbers for two different taxi services—the Cairns Cab Company and the Coral Sea Coach shuttle service.

Just last night, I'd gone online and made a two-night reservation at the Tropicana Lodge Motel, the least expensive motel I could find.

I'd been tracking exchange rates and weather reports (it was summer on the other side of the world, the days long and warm). I'd looked at transit maps and locations of Laundromats, in case I was there long enough to run out of clean clothes.

I'd memorized Australian phrases and learned that a *blue* is a fight, *to make a blue* is to make a mistake, and a *bluey* could either mean "dog," "jacket," "equipment," "redhead," or "Portuguese man-of-war."

I knew how to get from the airport to the motel, and how to get from the motel to Jamie's office.

I had planned so much, and I could picture the whole thing.

I mean, I could see myself there, starting from the moment I stepped off the plane into the warm Australian summer. I could picture shaking Jamie's hand, walking with him to the edge of the ocean. I could imagine calling my parents to tell them what I'd figured out.

The only thing I couldn't imagine was actually leaving home.

I glanced at Dr. Legs, who was doing that thing she does, where she folds her hands in her lap and stares out at nothing.

"I have a question," I said. At this point, so close to leaving, what did I have to lose by asking one question?

She seemed startled that I'd said anything, but she recovered quickly. She looked at me and smiled. "I'll be happy to answer it, Suzanne."

"How…"

I hesitated. I wanted to know how I could do this, how I could make this trip—how I might be able to walk out of my house, get on that plane, leave behind everyone I knew without hurting their feelings.

I tried again. "How…"

I shook my head. It was so hard to explain.

"Just ask, Suzanne," said Dr. Legs. "Whatever it is, it's okay."

"How…does a person say goodbye?"

It wasn't exactly the right question, but maybe it was close enough.

"Oh, Suzanne." Dr. Legs looked at me for a long time, and her face got soft. I swear, I thought she might cry, the way she was looking at me. "Are you ready to say goodbye?"

I shrugged.

"It's been, what, about six months?"

Six months since what? What was she even talking about?

And then I realized. *Oh. That.*

She pressed her lips together and shook her head, all the while keeping those soft eyes on me. "Saying goodbye is important," she said. "It's what allows us to begin living again."

I shifted in my seat. She wasn't exactly giving me instructions.

"There really are no magic words," said Dr. Legs. "There's no single right way to say goodbye to someone you love. But the most important thing is that you keep some part of them inside you."

I tried to imagine bringing some part of my family with me—all I could imagine were miniature versions of my mom, dad, Aaron, and Rocco, like tiny dolls that I could place in my pocket.

"In the end, Suzanne," Dr. Legs continued, "it's a gift to spend time with people we care about. Even if it's imperfect. Even if that time doesn't end when, or how, we expected. Even when that person leaves us."

Even when that person leaves us. But, of course, I was the one leaving. I imagined my mom coming home to an empty house. My dad waiting for me at Ming Palace, drinking his Rolling Rock. Maybe it would be a relief to all of them. They'd get a break from all my not-talking. Just for a little while, they wouldn't have me there smothering everything with my silence.

Dr. Legs narrowed her eyes and tilted her head. "Does that make sense, Suzanne?"

I really didn't know what made sense anymore.

Dr. Legs kept looking at me, which made me uncomfortable. So I said, "Sure. Yeah, I guess."

"I'm so proud of you, Suzanne," she said. "You've really come so far."

I haven't been anywhere, I wanted to say. *I haven't been anywhere at all.*

But that was about to change.

goodbye, ming palace

ON THE LAST SATURDAY BEFORE MY TRIP, MY
dad and I sat down in the pink vinyl booth at
Ming Palace just like we always did.

I was not like Bridget Brown. I'd done my
research. And I had learned four things:

1. Tuesday around 3 p.m., Eastern Standard
   Time, is the best time to find affordable
   airfare for international flights.
2. Flights that leave on Wednesday or
   Thursday tend to cost less than those that
   leave closer to weekends.

3. As it happened, my mom had an early-
   morning house showing this Thursday.
4. The moment I purchased my flight,
   it would be on my dad's credit card
   balance. And since I didn't know when
   he got his credit card statements, I
   needed to be careful. I needed to buy
   my ticket as close to the departure date
   as possible.

All of this meant that I would buy my ticket *this* Tuesday, 3 p.m. I would leave on Thursday morning.

I would be in Australia by Friday night, just as my classmates arrived at the Heroes and Villains dance.

By this point, I'd sat through twenty-one Ming Palace dinners since I'd started *not-talking*, which, at about an hour each, worked out to roughly 350,000 jellyfish stings.

And by this time next week, I'd be on the other side of the world.

I was just starting to wonder if they even had Chinese restaurants in Australia, when Dad said, "Oh, hey. I just read about something you might be interested in."

These days, Dad spoke to me the same way Rocco quoted dead writers—into the air, as if it didn't matter if anyone was listening at all.

I dipped a fried noodle into the little white bowl filled with duck sauce.

"Apparently there's a place not too far from here where they have real dinosaur tracks," Dad continued. "Hundreds and hundreds of footprints. Some guy driving a bulldozer discovered them by accident, and they built a whole museum around them."

He popped a crispy noodle into his mouth. "I thought maybe you and I could visit sometime."

No time soon, I thought. And then I felt a little wave of nausea.

The waitress set down our drinks. The ice in my Shirley Temple clinked against the glass.

"Sounds really cool," he said. He nodded at the

waitress as a kind of thank-you, then poured his beer. "We'd be able to walk where dinosaurs did. Apparently they were all over this whole valley."

I thought about that, considered that dinosaurs, real dinosaurs, had walked near where I now sat in a Chinese restaurant drinking a Shirley Temple, tens of millions of years later.

We ate. I watched the fish in the tank. Those poor fish didn't even know there was such a thing as a giant ocean tank in an aquarium, let alone an entire ocean. They probably thought this glass tank was the whole world.

When the server set down our fortune cookies at the end of the meal, mine was blank. The lucky numbers were on one side, just like they always are, and the LEARN CHINESE message told me that in Chinese, *winter* is *dong tian*.

But on the side where the fortune would go, there was just a line drawing of a rose—otherwise, it was totally blank.

I reached over to look at my dad's fortune. It said, A SMOOTH LONG JOURNEY! GREAT EXPECTATIONS.

I frowned, because it really seemed like that one should have been mine.

On the way home, we listened to the news. There were wildfires out west, landslides on the other side of the world. Doctors had spent fourteen hours removing a tumor that weighed more than the small girl whose body it had been growing in. I tried to picture this, a child-sized lump on top of an actual child, but I could only imagine a giant balloon, carrying her away.

And then I heard the announcer say a name I recognized: Diana Nyad.

"...is making final preparations for her fifth attempt to swim from Cuba to Florida without a shark tank," the announcer said. "Her previous attempts were foiled by jelly—"

Dad swerved around a car that had merged into his lane. "Sure, buddy," he muttered to the other driver. "It's all about you."

"Shhhhh," I hissed. I turned up the radio.

"The sixty-four-year-old Nyad says she hopes this mission, her fifth, will finally allow her to claim victory over the jellies."

And then the newscaster moved on to a different story, and my dad glanced at me, his hands still on the wheel.

"You following that story?" My dad sounded surprised.

I shrugged and looked out the window at the barren trees. Diana Nyad might be scary tough, but there was something about her that I really liked: the way she knew what she wanted and stopped at nothing to make it happen. She refused all limitations: distance, age, even jellyfish stings.

When we got to my mom's house, my dad said, "Good night, kiddo," like he always did.

I got out of the car just like I always did.

He waited in the driveway until I walked through

the front door. Just before I stepped inside, I waved to him.

Goodbye, Dad.

He flicked his headlights, then backed out of the driveway.

Here's the most important thing I've learned from *not-talking*: It is much, much easier to keep a secret when you don't use any words at all.

tuesday, 3 p.m.

AND THEN IT WAS TUESDAY.

The day I would buy my ticket using my dad's credit card.

Buying the ticket was simple enough. I plugged in my dates and locations. The ticket would take me to Chicago, then to Hong Kong, then to Brisbane.

It seemed impossible to imagine that my body would be in any of those places. From my tiny bedroom in South Grove, Massachusetts, none of those places seemed real at all.

My ticket would get me to Cairns, Australia, a

day and a half after I departed. I'd go from winter to summer in just thirty-six hours.

I typed in each number of the credit card, my dad's full name, the expiration date. Everything.

At the bottom of the travel site where I made my reservation was a big red button: PURCHASE TICKET.

I clicked it. Just like that.

And then it was real.

I sat and breathed for a while.

When I got up, I called the Green Hills Airport Shuttle. I said I needed to get to the airport for an international flight. I said it confidently, as if I booked travel plans like this all the time.

The voice on the other end of the line didn't register any surprise. The voice didn't ask me how old I was. The voice just asked me what time my flight was and then told me what time I should be picked up.

I had two choices. The shuttle could pick me up from the student center at the university where Aaron coached, or it could pick me up from a downtown hotel.

The university was riskier but closer. I could walk there.

I told them I'd take the campus shuttle.

They told me I needed $54 in cash.

It was arranged.

wednesday

IN SCHOOL THE NEXT DAY, MY LAST DAY THERE, I felt a strange sort of elation.

I am done with this.

I am leaving and I won't be back until I have proved something important.

It was like I was floating through the hallway. Like I was there and not-there at the same time. Almost like I was already a ghost. *Ghost heart.*

At the end of the day, Justin came over to my locker. "Hey, Belle," he said. "You coming to the dance Friday?"

And in that instant, I wanted so badly to tell him. Maybe if I'd needed someone to deliver a message after I left, I would have done it. But I wasn't completely sure he would keep his mouth shut. So I shook my head. "I'll be out of town."

"Too bad," he said. "I've got a great costume planned."

"What are you, a villain or a hero?" I asked, referring to the theme my classmates had chosen.

"Sorry," he said, and he smiled. "Gotta be at the dance to know for sure."

The bell rang. We put on our coats and walked to the buses together.

Just before I got on my bus, I paused and grinned right at him.

"What are you smiling about?" he asked.

"Villain," I said. "I'll bet your costume is a villain."

I got on my bus and sat in my seat alone. Justin waved at me through the window. Then he dug his hands deep into his coat pockets before walking off to board his own bus.

The engines started up, and I watched as Eugene Field Memorial Middle School got smaller and smaller, its bricks and cement gradually disappearing into the distance.

When I stepped off the school bus, I decided not to go straight home. Instead, I walked through the cold air to Aaron and Rocco's apartment. I wanted to hear them call me Suzy Q one last time. I wanted to be distracted by their energy and conversation. But when I rang the doorbell, no one answered.

I stood there in their backyard, watching my breath. My fingers were numb, and I longed to go inside, to sit in their space if I couldn't sit with them.

I knew they kept their key under a potted plant in the backyard. They probably wouldn't mind if I let myself in. Just for a few minutes. Just long enough to warm up before going home.

Inside, I wandered from room to room: the kitchen with its clean, still-wet dishes resting neatly in the dish rack (Aaron and Rocco couldn't have been gone long). The bathroom, which smelled of shaving cream. The living room with its stacks of magazines, *Sports Illustrated* and the *New Yorker* and the *Atlantic* and something called *Adbusters*. In the corner, a pair of Nike sneakers with inside-out athletic socks stuffed into them.

I hated that I was leaving them.

On the mantel I saw a framed photograph of Aaron from years ago, resting on top of some cash. A Post-it note was stuck to the frame.

I lifted the picture. In it, Aaron stood on a soccer field, the same field I saw every day through the window of my math class. He held a soccer ball and wore thick glasses and had braces—I'd forgotten that he'd ever worn braces. His arms looked so skinny— skinnier even than mine. He must have been my age when this photograph was taken.

I saw no trace of the confident coach he was today.

On the note, Rocco had written, *I loved you before I knew you. Even when you looked like this. XOXO.*

I placed the picture back on the mantel, and I

picked up the money. Two twenties, a five, and three ones. Forty-eight dollars.

I'd already taken so much from my mom. I had booked a flight on my dad's credit card. I didn't need to steal from these guys, too, did I?

And yet. I didn't really know *what* I needed. What if I was short by exactly $48?

I thought about Bridget Brown standing in the Nashville airport, counting her money.

I stuffed the cash into the pocket of my jeans, started for the door, and then paused.

I ran back to the mantel, grabbed the framed photo of Aaron, and ran out of the apartment. It was only after I stepped outside that I realized I'd left the key inside, on the mantel. I turned back to get it, but their door had locked from the inside. I was locked out.

I didn't know what else to do, so I ran practically the whole way home, gripping Aaron's photo and nearly slipping several times on the icy sidewalk.

goodbye, home

IT WAS THURSDAY, 7:18 A.M. MY LAST MORNING at home. Mom would leave early this morning, thinking I'd catch the school bus on my own. But instead of going to school, I'd head to campus, so the shuttle could take me to the airport.

I was placing slices of bread in our broken old toaster, another one of Mom's thrift-store "treasures," when she walked into the kitchen, wearing her work clothes. She kissed me on top of my head, and I pulled away.

"You remember that I've got a showing this morning, right, Zu?"

Of course I did. I had arranged my plans around it.

"You have everything you need for the day?"

I nodded. I did, although it wasn't exactly the day she thought I had planned.

Mom picked up her bag, started sorting through papers. "Ugh," she said. "I just hate showing houses in the winter. Everything always looks so bleak."

In my head I told her. *I am going, Mom. I am going away.*

As Mom shoved the papers back into her bag, I opened the utensil drawer and pulled out a butter knife.

"I don't know," she mused. "Maybe summer's not *that* far away."

I shut the drawer harder than I'd intended.

"Whoa, careful there," she snapped.

I am sorry, Mom. You will not understand.

When my toast popped up, the edges were blackened.

Stupid burned toast from this stupid so-called treasure. Somehow, those black edges seemed like the saddest thing in the world.

And then I got angry at myself about being sad.

Sad was dangerous. Sad could ruin everything. Sad was the one thing that might still stop me.

I threw the toast into the sink, hard. Crumbs scattered all over the metal basin.

"Zu," my mom said. She sounded surprised.

I ripped open the bag of bread and yanked out two more slices.

Just go, just go, just go. I can't get started until you go away.

Mom shook her head. "Whoa," she muttered. "Someone got up on the wrong side of the bed."

I placed the bread in the toaster and turned the dial down to the lightest setting. From behind me, my mom put her hands on my shoulders. I ducked away from her touch.

Mom, just go. You're the last one I have to say goodbye to, and I just want this part to be over. Please, just go.

I threw open the refrigerator door. The bottles and jars inside the door rattled.

"Okay, Zu," Mom said. "What is up with you today?"

What is up with me is that I am about to do this very big thing. And every moment you spend with me makes me want to do it less.

I stared inside the fridge for a second.

"What are you looking for?" she asked. "Butter?"

And that is why I need you to disappear.

I slammed the refrigerator door shut. More glass rattled.

My mom took a deep breath—the kind where she breathes in and out through her nose, really, really slowly. I knew she was trying to avoid what she would call *losing her cool*.

She walked to the refrigerator and opened the door. Then, without saying a word, she placed a stick of butter, the wrapper half-open, on the counter in front of me.

I didn't dare look at her. Instead, I brought the butter to my nose, as if I were sniffing it. I tossed it back onto the counter like it smelled bad.

"For heaven's sake, Zu. You're being rude."

Please. Please, just go.

My toast popped up, less burned this time. I

grabbed it, slammed it onto a plate, and started smearing butter on it so hard that I ripped the bread.

"Zu," Mom said, "if there's something I can do to help turn your morning around, this would be the time to tell me."

And then I said it.

"Just go," I muttered.

"Zu..."

I whipped around, the hiss already coming out of me. "Just go, Mom. I don't. Want. You. Here."

I wanted to be past this part. I wanted to have already crawled through my escape hatch into whatever world lay beyond. I wanted all the goodbyes to be over with.

Mom glanced at the clock. "I don't want to be late, but, honey—"

"What is *wrong* with you?" I cut her off. "Why can't you just *go away?*"

There was such a gulf between my insides and outsides, between what was in my heart and what I was putting into the world. That gulf was so big it was about to crack me into three billion pieces, right there in the middle of the kitchen.

Mom took a deep breath. "I don't know what to do," she said softly.

"You should go," I said. "That's what you should do."

Mom picked up her bag. "I'll see you after school, okay?" she said. "We can talk then."

I won't be here, Mom. I'm sorry, but I won't be here. There is something I have to do.

"I hope your day gets better from here, Zu." She paused, then added, "I love you."

She closed the door quietly behind her.

As I listened to her footsteps on the walk, I wanted two things at once: I wanted to make my escape. But at the same time, I wanted to chase my mom so she could stop me from leaving. I wanted her to tell me that there were people who needed me here, at home, more than anyone else needed me to do this thing.

I wanted her to put me to bed, and to wake me only when everything was back to normal.

But I didn't know anymore what normal even looked like.

Mom's car drove away.

It was only when she was gone that I understood I still had one more goodbye.

phone call

I PICKED UP THE PHONE.

I still knew the number by heart, remembered it from years of can't-wait conversations, like the time we both finished reading *James and the Giant Peach* on the same day and I couldn't wait to talk to her about the peach mansion in New York City. Or the hundreds of times we called each other to check the homework assignment, even though we both already knew it. Or the day Dylan Parker showed up at school with his high-top sneakers and Patriots jersey and his hair spiked into a faux-hawk and Franny called to say, "That new kid is really weird,

right?" I hadn't noticed he was particularly weird—
I hadn't given him much thought at all—but I said
yes, and then didn't figure out for a long time why
she'd wanted to talk about him in the first place.

The phone rang three times. I was just about to
hang up when I heard someone pick up.

"Hello?"

Franny's mom.

I took a deep breath. She couldn't have known
that I'd spent the last few months *not-talking*, that
I'd not spoken into a phone since before Franny
died. She couldn't have known how hard it was to
say anything at all.

"How is Fluffernutter?"

There was a long pause before Franny's mom
answered.

"She's good, Suzy," she said. "You can come over
and play with her sometime if you want."

I thought about that. I imagined going over
there and sitting with Franny's mom, instead of her
alone, and me alone, the two of us connected only by
some cords strung up on wooden posts along the side

of the roads. I wasn't sure I would ever want that, but I said, "Okay."

We didn't say anything for a while. Then I said, "Maybe it's too early in the day to call. I didn't think about that."

"No, it's fine. I've been up for a while." I pictured her sitting in the kitchen, the wallpaper border near the ceiling with its strips of stamped ivy, the floral porcelain handles on the cabinets. Franny and I always smeared brownie batter on those handles when we baked, no matter how hard we tried to keep everything neat.

"There's a school dance tomorrow night."

"Yeah?"

"Yeah. The theme is heroes and villains."

It was hard to know what was okay to say and what wasn't. I mean, maybe I shouldn't even have told her about the dance, since Franny never got a chance to go to any dances. It was weird. I was growing, and other kids were growing. In a few months, I would officially be a teenager. In another year, I would be nearly fourteen years old, which sounded so old it seemed nearly impossible. But Franny would always be twelve.

"Which are you?" Franny's mom asked.

"What?"

"Are you going as a hero or a villain?"

"Oh," I said. "I won't be there. I'll be out of town."

I took a deep breath, because this was it: This was my chance to explain everything I was about to do and why. To tell her that everyone else might have given up at *sometimes things just happen*. But I hadn't.

Before I had a chance to begin, Franny's mom said, "You know she always admired you so much, Suzy."

And then I didn't know *what* to say.

"She said you never cared what anyone else thought. I could tell how much she liked that about you. I think she wished she had a little more of that in her."

Franny's mom's words were such a surprise that I wondered if she might be lying.

It had never occurred to me that Franny might

wish she could be like me. And of course what Franny's mom had just said wasn't true: I *had* cared what someone thought. I'd cared what Franny thought.

We just sat there for a while, each in our different homes, *not-talking* with each other.

It's peculiar how no-words can be better than words. Silence can say more than noise, in the same way that a person's absence can occupy even more space than their presence did.

After a while, I bit my lip. "I have to go," I said.

"Thank you for calling, Suzy."

"Give Fluffernutter a kiss for me."

"I will. You take care of yourself, okay?"

I nodded, even though I knew she couldn't see me. Then we sat for another moment, until I heard something. It might have been the word *Bye*, but it also might have just been a tiny, sad little noise escaping from Franny's mom's throat.

I hung up the phone. I went to my bedroom and pulled my suitcase out of my closet. I placed the framed photograph of Aaron in the outer pocket. Then I picked the bag up and walked out the door.

endings

WHO KNOWS. MAYBE EVERYBODY'S END isn't the day they actually die, but the last time anyone speaks of them. Maybe when you die you don't really disappear, but you fade into a shadow, dark and featureless, only your outlines visible. Over time, as people forget you, your silhouette gradually fades into darkness until the final time anyone says your name on this planet. That's when your very last feature—the freckled tip of your nose, or the heart-top bubble of your lips—fades for good.

If that is true, it is a good reason to hold off saying someone's name after they die. Because you never know. You never know which time you say it might be the last time.

And then they will disappear for good.

part six

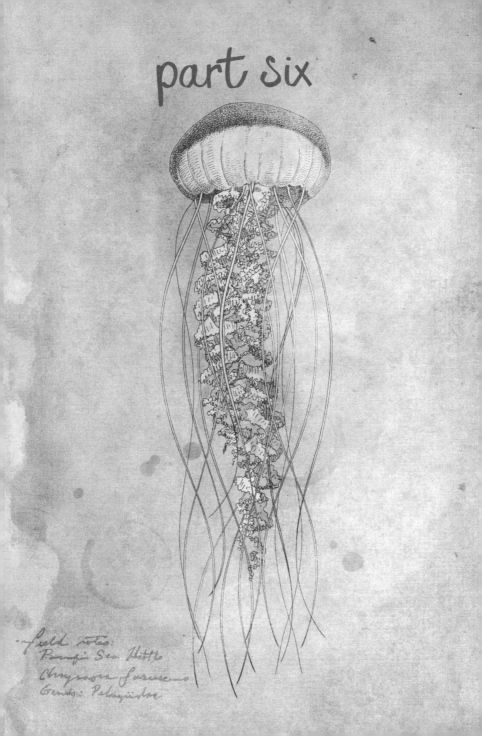

field notes:
Pacific Sea Nettle
Chrysaora fuscescens
Genus: Pelagiidae

Results

Summarize your observations. Do your outcomes support your hypothesis? Remember that science never actually "proves" anything; it merely contributes to a growing body of evidence about the way our world works. If your research does not appear to support your hypothesis, be honest about that. Remember that in science we learn as much from failures as we do from successes.

—MRS. TURTON

immortality

Here is the last, most important thing about jellyfish.

I'll bet you could never in a million years guess this one.

They are immortal.

I'm not exaggerating when I say that. I also don't just mean that they will outlast us, even though they will.

I mean it literally: There is at least one species of jellyfish that can grow younger, which is something that pretty much no other creature on Earth can do. Don't believe me? Look it up. *Turritopsis dohrnii.* The immortal jellyfish.

When it's threatened, *Turritopsis dohrnii* can return from its adult medusa stage, the stage where a jellyfish looks like a jellyfish, all the way back into a younger stage, where it clings to the bottom of the ocean floor for safety. Theoretically, it can do this indefinitely: grow old, then young, old, then young, and never really die.

It would be as if, when everything started going wrong, when it started getting stressful, we could have just gone backward. Imagine that. Imagine if we could have said, "Oops, this is too hard," and shrunk in size, returned to a place of being just kids, the way we always had been.

And we could just stay there, tethered safely, forever.

Then none of it would have happened like it did. I'd never have had to do anything to try to fix all those things that had gone wrong. I'd never have tried to send you that message. Everything would be okay. It would be easy, just like it used to be.

You would still be here. And, Franny, you would love me again. Just like you always did.

to australia

THE TRICK TO ANYTHING IS JUST BELIEVING you can do it. When you believe in your own ability to do something, even something scary, it gives you an almost magic power. Confidence *is* magic. It can carry you through everything.

It can carry you through a long walk to campus, dragging your suitcase as you go. It can carry you through the long, cold moments standing there, trying to look like you belong. It can carry you through the wondering: Is the shuttle really going to show up? And also the relief and fear you feel when it actually does.

The shuttle was filled with strangers. There was a woman with white hair who talked for a long time to a woman in a red business suit. White Hair said she was going to visit her brand-new grandson, *9 pounds 2 ounces*, in Atlanta. Red Suit replied that she was flying to Grand Rapids for one day—*just a quick in and out*—to deliver a talk on art conservation.

I made a point to not look at anyone. I did not make eye contact. Even when the shuttle stopped at a hotel and a man who smelled like old cigarettes sat next to me and said hello, I did not turn to look.

I watched the houses go by, and I thought, *Goodbye, houses.*

I watched the small roads turn into bigger roads, and I thought, *Goodbye, smaller roads.*

I watched the bigger roads give way to the highway, and I thought, *Goodbye, South Grove, Massachusetts.*

I reached into my coat pocket and ran my fingers over the pink index card, the one with my dad's credit card information.

So far, this had all been very easy. I felt proud of how well I'd planned.

I tried not to think about my mother, about the fact that I hadn't even hugged her goodbye. Instead, I'd just watched her get into her car and drive away.

When the shuttle arrived at the airport, passengers stepped out, one by one, at their different terminals. Each time, the open door sent a blast of arctic air into the shuttle. I noticed that they all seemed to hand the driver money before saying goodbye. So when we pulled up to the international terminal, I reached into my envelope and pulled out a crumpled dollar bill. I handed it to him, took my bag from him, and said thank you. The whole time, I looked coolly into the distance, as if I did this sort of thing every day.

And then I walked to the counter and waited in line.

Now I would get my boarding pass, walk through security, then fly to the edge of the world.

I had already set my watch to Cairns time, which was fifteen hours ahead of Massachusetts time.

I had a toothbrush in my small carry-on, along with a tiny tube of toothpaste.

I had a change of socks and a change of underwear, too, because I didn't want to arrive in Australia feeling too dirty.

I had a notebook filled with words and phrases I might need in Australia: *chemist* means "pharmacy," *boot* means "trunk," *lift* means "elevator," and *to come good* means "to turn out okay."

The first part of my journey had already come good.

I had Jamie Seymour's office address at James Cook University, which is about 15 kilometers, or 9 miles, from the airport. To get there, I would travel along the highway that is also named for Captain Cook, who, I knew from studying explorers with Franny, sailed from England to Australia. He traveled there nearly 250 years ago, as part of a long journey to see Venus cross between Earth and the sun.

Both those journeys—Cook's and Venus's—seemed to come good.

When I arrived, I would be less than a mile from

the ocean. I wondered if I would be able to hear the waves and if they would sound like the Earth breathing.

The passenger at the front of the line walked toward the gates, boarding pass in hand. Everyone in line, myself included, shuffled forward a couple of steps.

Australia was so close I could almost feel it.

sit

WALKING UP TO THE AIRPORT COUNTER, I made a point not to blink too much. Blinking means you're nervous. Nervous is suspicious.

The woman behind the counter had long blonde hair, and her eyes looked like they were set ever-so-slightly too far apart. She typed away on a keyboard, red nails tap-tapping in rapid fire.

"Name?"

I told her. She typed it in without looking up. *Tap tap tap.*

"Passport?"

I reached into my bag and handed it to her. The

woman opened up my passport, flipped through the empty pages. Then she frowned. "Wait," she said. "What's your date of birth?"

When I told her, she looked at me strangely. "Well, that doesn't..." she started, before her voice drifted off. She tapped a few more keys, then frowned. "And it looks like you haven't applied for a visa."

I wasn't entirely sure what she was talking about, but I knew, somehow, that the trip was starting to slip away from me.

Visa, I thought. *She said visa.*

Even as I understood that this wasn't going to fix anything, I did the only thing I could do: I reached into my pocket and pulled out the pink index card with my dad's credit card information. I slid it across the counter to her.

She looked at it, turned it over a few times. She seemed confused. "What is this?" she asked.

"It's a Visa," I said. I lifted my chin in the air and said it confidently, as though my brain weren't racing. *Just get past this moment*, I thought. *Do whatever you can to get on that plane.*

She frowned. "This is just..." She stared at it for a while, and then said, "Oh. Oh, I see."

She lifted her eyes. "Sweetie?" she asked. Her voice was suddenly very quiet. "Where are your parents?"

I took a deep breath and spoke with as much dignity as I could muster. "They are unable to make this trip," I said. I watched luggage roll past on a conveyor belt behind her.

I blinked a few times and added, "They both work."

She looked back down at the index card, like she was thinking about something. Then she said, "Honey, you know you can't fly out of the country by yourself."

"I purchased a ticket," I said.

"Yes, but—"

I quoted the Bridget Brown newspaper story. "Passengers ages twelve and over may travel with no adult supervision as long as they have a valid boarding pass."

"No," she said. "Not international travel."

When she spoke again, her voice was extremely quiet. "I'm sorry," she said.

It was the quiet that got to me, the fact that she was trying so hard to be kind. If she thought I needed kindness, it wasn't a good sign.

The thing is, not doing this, not making this trip, wasn't an option. Not anymore.

I looked down, trying to figure out what to say next. I knew what needed to happen now: I needed to regain control of this situation, and fast. There was a crowd of travelers behind me, and I didn't have much time.

I stared at the swirly pattern on the laminate countertop. But for the life of me, I could not figure out how to take back control.

Then something inside me understood, *This is not going to work.*

That was when the swirls disappeared into a blur. My hands, the index card, my expired passport, dissolved into ripples. I saw a fat drop land on the counter.

"Oh, hon," the lady said.

I heard the whir of the airport around me. Heard footsteps and rolling luggage carts. Beyond those sounds, I heard the hum of the building: the heating system, maybe. Or maybe the fluorescent lights. I wondered, if I listened hard enough, if I might be able to hear my own blood pumping through my body.

I realized I was shaking.

I thought about Bridget Brown, who flew to Tennessee and then had to turn around and go home. *At least she got to go somewhere*, I thought.

I had gotten only as far as the ticket counter.

I felt a hand on my shoulder. The lady had come out from behind the counter. Standing next to me, she was smaller than I'd expected. Even wearing heels, she wasn't any bigger than I was.

"Come with me," she said.

I let her guide me around to the side of the counter, the place where the employees go in and out.

"Sit," she said. I dropped to the floor.

I looked up at her, saw the way she was looking at me, and then she got all blurry, too. Hot tears started rolling down my face.

She squatted down next to me, placed one hand on my arm, and gave me a small squeeze. Then she stood up and walked away. I put my head against my knees, pressing my eyes right into my kneecaps.

I was tired. The light hurt.

I had failed.

she made it

I SAT ON THE FLOOR FOR A LONG TIME, WATCHING people check in at the counter and head off toward their gates.

I saw a man with white hair and neon-orange sneakers. A woman soldier, all in camouflage. A mom with a toddler. The kid had snot running down his face and was crying in a whiny, tired way. He was wearing a sweatshirt, and his mom kept putting his hood on. Each time she did, he ripped it off. She jiggled him on her hip and stared straight ahead.

All of these people were going somewhere.

I shut my eyes and focused on my breath. I'd been breathing all day, all week, all my life, and I had forgotten to notice until now.

Franny was never coming back.

That was the thing. Even if I could get Jamie to tell me that the problem had been a jellyfish, that I'd been right all along, it wouldn't change anything. Franny would still be gone, and our friendship would still have ended how it ended.

I am sorry. I am sorry. I am so very, very sorry.

My eyes still closed, I listened to the boy crying, to the tapping of the airline keyboards, to the loudspeaker calling out that the luggage from the Toronto flight would soon be arriving on carousel three.

I am sorry I wasn't who you wanted me to be. I am sorry about what I did. I'm sorry for whatever you must have experienced in that awful moment when you disappeared.

A cell phone had been found in the women's restroom and could be retrieved on the lower level.

I am sorry I am just a dumb creature on a rock

hurtling through space. I'm sorry I made your time on this rock, this stupid little mote of dust, harder and not easier.

I'm sorry that my attempt at a new beginning turned out to be the very worst kind of ending.

I'm sorry I got so much so wrong.

I must have fallen asleep, because when I opened my eyes, there were blankets on top of me, several of those thin, fleecy airline squares. They were placed in a kind of patchwork so that every part of me was covered. I looked up, but I didn't see the blonde airline lady anywhere. A man in a suit jogged past, dragging a black bag that rolled behind him like a reluctant dog.

I lay down and curled into a ball, adjusting the blankets over me. The floor was hard and cold, and it felt good against my cheek.

I closed my eyes again.

The next time I opened them, my mom was there.

It was such a surprise to see her, in this airport with all these strangers. She still wore the house-showing clothes that she'd had on during those final moments in the kitchen.

Mom's eyes searched my face. She looked sort of panicked.

"Zu," Mom said. She sank down onto the floor next to me. "Oh honey." Her face crumpled, and tears began streaming down her cheeks.

I didn't know if they were love tears or sad tears or happy tears or all three at once.

"Oh. Oh, my sweet, sweet Zu." She took my hands and squeezed them tight.

Then Aaron was there, too. He sat, made a soft fist, and bumped me on the knee.

Nobody spoke for a long time.

Then, after a while, Aaron said, all casual, "So...what's going on, Zu?" And the way he said it—as if this whole situation were completely normal—made me laugh a little. Snot shot out of my nose, but I didn't care. I wiped my nose with the back of my hand.

"I thought..." I started. I took a deep breath. "I thought I could prove it," I said. "I thought I could prove what really happened."

But of course they didn't know what I was talking about. They didn't know about any of the things I'd been thinking about for the last few months. They didn't know about the trip to the aquarium, or the Irukandji, or the twenty-three-stings-every-five-seconds. They didn't know about Jamie, or my research, or how I thought I'd figured out something that no one else had. They didn't know about Bridget Brown and Dollywood, or about any of the things that had led to my sitting alone on an airport floor.

They didn't understand how something impossible could become the only possible thing.

I listened to the words tumbling out of me, more words than I'd said in a long, long time. I could hear that they made no sense. No matter how hard I tried to explain, I couldn't make my explanation sound any more reasonable.

It occurred to me that maybe this is another thing that happens when you stop talking. Maybe you lose track of whether the things inside your head are normal and reasonable or filled with cracks and flaws.

When I was done, when all the words were out and I'd explained as best I could, I remembered what Dr. Legs had said the very first time I met her—that everybody grieves in different ways, that there's no right or wrong way to grieve.

Well, I thought. *When she hears about this, she may just change her mind.*

When I was done speaking, we sat for a few minutes. Then my mother said quietly, "I always figured it was a riptide."

I looked at her. "What?"

"I mean—I don't know why she drowned, Zu. But that's what I always assumed. That it was a riptide."

A riptide. An invisible current that pulls a person out to sea.

"It could have been anything, though," Mom said. Her voice was so gentle. "I mean, maybe Franny got tossed by a wave and hit her head on a rock. Or maybe it was a medical thing—like a seizure, or she had a heart problem that no one knew about. Or maybe she was just a little too tired, and swam just a little too far from shore...."

Her voice trailed off.

She didn't say what she could have, and neither did Aaron. Neither of them told me what I suddenly understood—that whatever it was, whatever the reason, it didn't really matter. It *had* "just happened."

Somehow, that fact—that sometimes things *do* just happen—seemed like it might be the scariest and saddest truth of all.

Then I saw Rocco approaching, holding a cardboard tray of hot drinks. He handed my mom a cup, then offered one to me. "Cocoa, Suzy?"

On the cup was a picture of a green mermaid, long hair cascading over her chest. There was a crown on her head, with a star on top. Sea and sky meeting on a cardboard cup. Even though it was just a dumb old logo, it still felt like Rocco had just handed me a message, something that said, *We understand.*

The cocoa was delicious. For a while, we simply sat there on the floor, sipping our drinks and not-talking.

Then I saw my envelope of money peeking out of the suitcase. "I stole," I said, and the words felt terrible coming out of my mouth. "I used Dad's credit card."

Then I picked up the envelope of cash and handed it to my mom. "And a lot of this is yours," I said. I turned to Aaron and Rocco. "But some of it is yours."

I explained about taking the money from their living room.

"We already knew, Zu," Aaron said. He glanced at Rocco. "We had a fight about it, actually. It was his portion of the grocery money. Rocco swore he'd left it there for me, and I swore he couldn't have, because it wasn't there. Then we noticed the picture missing, and the key sitting there. That was the only explanation."

I looked down at the floor. "I'm sorry." I was surprised by how small my voice sounded, how young.

Rocco, who had missed my explanation, asked, "Was it for a good cause?"

"It was," said Aaron.

Rocco placed a hand on mine. "You know, there are worse misdeeds than those that are done for a higher purpose."

I wiped my nose. "Who said that?"

"What do you mean?" he asked.

"Is that a quote?"

He shook his head. "No, Suzy Q. It's just the truth."

I lay down with my head on my mom's lap, which was warmer and softer than I remembered. It reminded me of a fact from Jenna's presentation—that a mother dolphin does not stop swimming for the first several weeks of her newborn's life. The newborn calf doesn't have enough blubber to float, so it needs to be carried along in its mother's slipstream. If the mother stops swimming, even for a short time, the calf will sink.

It must be tiring, being a mom.

At a nearby waiting area, I noticed a television running a news clip of a beach full of people holding up cameras and phones. Whatever was happening, they all wanted to record it. Close to shore, three kayaks followed an object that bobbed in the water.

It was a person. A person swimming toward shore.

Some words appeared: HISTORIC CUBA-FLORIDA SWIM.

I stood.

NYAD COMPLETES 103-MILE SWIM ON FIFTH ATTEMPT.

Without even thinking, I began moving toward the television.

"Oh," Mom said, following me. "I read about this."

Diana Nyad was just a few yards from shore. Just a few more strokes to go. If she stood now, she could walk right out of that water.

"Wow," Rocco said. "She made it."

He whistled through his teeth. "Fifth time's the charm, I guess."

Nyad hovered in the water, not moving at all. Then she slowly stood and stumbled forward, her steps so stilted it was almost as if she couldn't remember how to walk. All around her, supporters held their arms out, ready to grab her if she fell. But they let her take those final steps out of the water unaided.

The crowd applauded wildly.

"She's so brave," I murmured.

We watched quietly as EMTs helped Nyad into an ambulance, and the ambulance drove slowly away from the beach. The crowd walked behind the ambulance, still cheering.

That's when Aaron turned to me.

"Zu?"

"Yeah?"

"Can we take you home now?"

I felt my face crumple, felt the tears again, but this time they weren't just sad tears. They were the other kind, too. The love kind.

The four of us walked toward the parking garage.

When the sliding door opened and we stepped outside, there was a great burst of traffic and cold air and bright light. It hit me hard, as if I'd been holding my breath underwater and I'd finally lifted my head above the surface.

It was like gulping fresh air for the first time in a long time.

part seven

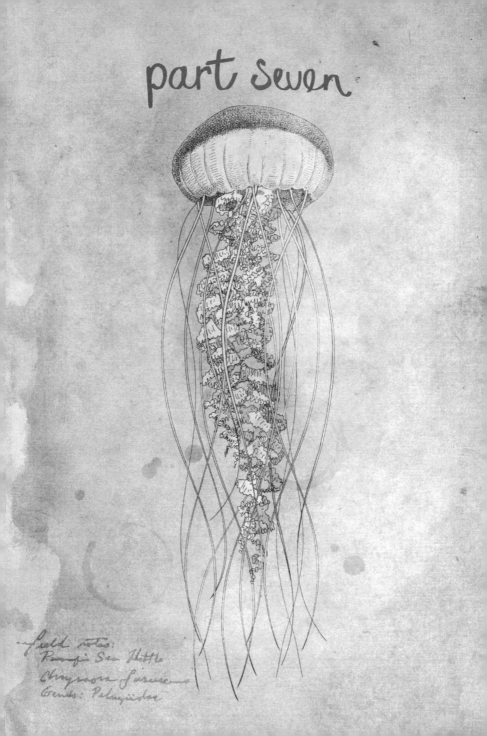

field notes:
Pacific Sea Nettle
Chrysaora fuscescens
Genus: Pelagiidae

Conclusion

What did you learn from your research? Take a step beyond your own investigation to consider the implications for future questions. What else is there to learn? Where might your inquiry take you next?

—MRS. TURTON

what if?

THEY ARE STILL OUT THERE, THOSE JELLYFISH. They are still out there with their twenty-three stings every five seconds. They will be out there for the rest of my life. Maybe even for the rest of life on Earth.

I think about the immortal jellyfish, the one that can grow younger. I wonder: Is it possible that there is more than one way to grow younger? Is there some way humans can grow younger, too?

Like, what if we could return to the feeling we had when we were little, that sense that anything is possible?

Back in 1968, people saw Earth rising over the

moon and believed they mattered. They believed they could accomplish anything.

What if we could feel that way again?

There are so many things to be scared of in this world: blooms of jellies. A sixth extinction. A middle school dance. But maybe we can stop feeling so afraid. Maybe instead of feeling like a mote of dust, we can remember that all the creatures on this Earth are made from stardust.

And we are the only ones who get to *know* it.

That's the thing about jellyfish: They'll never understand that. All they can do is drift along, unaware.

Humans may be newcomers to this planet. We may be plenty fragile. But we're also the only ones who can decide to change.

the only thing that ever made sense

THAT EVENING WAS A FLURRY OF PHONE CALLS.
My mom called my dad to tell him what
happened. My dad and my mom got on a confer-
ence call with the credit card company first, and then
with the airline. I listened as they were transferred
from person to person.

I heard my mom tell the story over and over again,
stopping occasionally to say things like *That's right.*
Twelve. She made the reservation online. Yes, by herself.
No. No, I didn't know.

I slept hard that night. In the morning, my mom
didn't wake me for school. I was glad about that. If

Mom had any house-showing appointments, she must have canceled them, because when I finally came downstairs for breakfast, she was standing in the kitchen in flannel pajamas. She had the phone cradled to one ear, a steaming cup of coffee in her hand.

"Great," she said into the phone. She winked at me. She looked tired, like she hadn't slept much at all.

"Great," she said again. "You've been so helpful. Thanks."

She hung up the phone. "Good news, Zu," she said. "The airline is going to refund the charge to Dad's credit card."

I looked at the floor.

"All of it?"

"All of it." Then she muttered under her breath, almost as much to herself as to me, "They should, too. They can't sell a ticket to a twelve-year-old."

I walked outside, still in my pajamas, and watched my breath in the cold air.

If things had gone as planned, I would have been

arriving in Cairns right about now. I'd probably be checking into the Tropicana Lodge Motel at this very second. It would be nighttime now, and summer.

And here I was, in Massachusetts on a winter morning, shivering in my pj's on the front stoop of the only house I'd ever known.

When I really thought about it, that was the only thing that made any sense.

Mom appeared in the doorway. "Zu? I think you owe your dad a phone call."

I shook of my head.

"Honey," she said. "He and I talked last night, and again this morning. He's upset, but honestly he's more worried than anything."

But I couldn't call. Not yet.

I mean, how does a person just begin again, especially after all that?

any other kid

I DIDN'T PLAN TO GO TO THE HEROES AND VIL-lains school dance. I didn't think about the dance all day long. Not when Aaron and Rocco stopped by with lunch. Not when Aaron turned on a soccer match, and we all watched as a team called Liverpool beat a team called Tottenham in the final minutes of the game. Not after they left, while my mom made chicken with rice, which is my favorite.

But as I was eating, the phone rang.

Mom picked it up. A moment later, she shook her head. "I'm afraid you have the wrong number," she said. "There's no Belle—"

I looked up then, eyes wide.

A second later, she laughed. "Oh, *Suzy*. Okay, sure, she's here.... No, she's not out of town."

She winked at me. "She was away, but she's back now.... Yeah, okay, hold on."

She raised one eyebrow and looked at me slyly. "Someone named Justin would like to speak to you, Zu."

She waved the phone at me and mouthed the words *Come on*.

But I didn't take the phone from her. She sighed.

"She can't come to the phone right this second. Is there a—? Got it. Okay. Yes, I got it. *Awesomesauce*. Right. I'll tell her."

She hung up the phone and gave me a funny look. "*Justin*"—she emphasized his name—"has asked me to tell you that his costume for the dance is 'awesomesauce.' He hopes you'll come so you can see it."

The Heroes and Villains dance. Of course. That was tonight. My stomach did a little flip-flop just thinking about all that music. All those kids.

Mom leaned in. "Who is Justin?"

"He's a—"

I thought for a moment, not sure how to describe him. "Well," I said. "He's ... a friend, I guess."

The word felt funny in my mouth, but as soon as I said it, I knew it was true.

Somehow, that was enough.

It didn't take long for me to get my costume together. I walked into Aaron's room, opened his closet door, and found an old paint-splattered Red Sox cap— the one he wore a few summers ago when he helped paint houses and came home every evening covered in green and yellow drips. I also grabbed a gray T-shirt with a pocket. It was long enough to be like a dress on me, and it actually looked pretty good over a pair of leggings.

I went into my room and sat on my bed. My suitcase was on the floor, still packed. Just seeing it there gave me the same feeling inside that listening to my mom talking on the phone had: like I was very, very young.

I reached down and pulled out the photo of Aaron, the one I'd swiped from Aaron and Rocco's apartment. It was nice, in a way, knowing that he'd once been so young and weird-looking.

Maybe he'd once felt like an outsider in his own life, too.

I took the picture out of its frame and placed it in the pocket of the T-shirt.

Then I took a deep breath, went downstairs, and asked my mom if she could drive me to school.

what remains

IF IT'S TRUE WHAT SOME SCIENTISTS THINK—
that all moments in time exist simultaneously—then
this is real, and it is happening now, just as it happened
before:

We are under the big tree in my backyard, on that
patch of dirt where we used to build fairy houses from
moss and sticks and scraps of birch. It is late afternoon.
All around us is golden light.

We have been together all day, in our cutoff shorts and
bare feet.

It is the start of fifth grade, the start of being the oldest
in the school. Next year, we will be the youngest all over
again. But not yet.

We are playing that hand-slapping game, the one we like to play at recess. You hold your hands out, palms up, and I place mine lightly on top. You pull yours out and try to slap mine. You hit air three times. On the fourth try, your hands make contact with mine.

We laugh.

I hold my palms faceup, and your hands touch mine, ready to pull back. I can feel the heat of your fingers, which is the heat of your blood pulsing through your veins.

Your face blocks the sun, which hangs low in the sky. The edges of your face, your arms, glow white. It is as if someone has traced you with a glow-in-the-dark marker. You shift, and the afternoon's rays break through from behind your head. I squint, and you disappear into a silhouette. You shift again, and there you are again, your freckles, your light hair glowing like a halo.

I move my hands, and you pull yours away, just in time. Our laughter escapes from us, unnoticed. It floats into that golden light around us. If we tried, we could reach out and grab that laughter, the way a person can catch sparks flying out from a campfire, or dandelion seeds carried by the wind. We could squeeze that laughter in our hands, feel its warmth, like stones that hold the day's heat on a summer evening.

I move again, and just graze the top of your hands.

"Missed," you say.

And I say, "I got you."

And you say, "Nunh- uh."

And I say, "Yah-huh." Then we do it again, and I get you this time, and our laughter makes us round our shoulders. Our shadows grow longer as the sun sinks toward the horizon.

Our knees touch. We begin again.

heroes and villains

SITTING IN MY MOTHER'S CAR, I WATCHED AS kids streamed into the building in their heroes and villains costumes. I saw several Harry Potters and just as many Voldemorts. There were Katniss Everdeens, a bunch of classic superhero types with capes and tights, and a couple of masked men, dressed in black, like the kind of bad guys you'd see in an old Western movie. Dylan Parker walked past dressed as a priest, of all things.

I didn't get out of the car.

"Hon?" Mom asked. "You okay?"

Two kids—both dressed as Avengers—passed in front of our car.

I imagined the gym, dark and covered with streamers.

What had I been thinking, coming here?

"I think I want to go home," I said.

Mom sighed. Then she reached into her purse and dug out her phone. She pressed it into my hands.

But I still didn't get out of the car.

"Suzy," she said. "How long does it take to get from here to the house?"

A Batman and a Joker walked past. I couldn't tell who they were.

"Zu?" Mom said. "How many minutes?"

"I dunno," I said. "Maybe five minutes?"

"And how many seconds is five minutes?" she asked.

"Three hundred."

"Right," she said. "So here's what I want you to do: I want you to walk in there and give this dance at least three hundred seconds. If you really can't stand it, you can use this phone to call me. I'll come get you. Okay? But at least walk through that door, Zu."

Three hundred seconds. That was all she was asking.

"Honey, just yesterday you were ready to fly to another continent."

Yes, but I failed.

She took my chin in her hands and looked in my eyes, just for a moment. "You are brave, Zu. Braver than anyone I know. You can do this."

I squeezed my eyes shut so that I wouldn't start crying all over again.

When I opened them, I looked down at the phone in my hands. I wanted so much to be able to do this—for Mom's sake, even more than for my own.

Then, as if she could read my mind, she said, "For me, Zu? Please just give it a try?"

I pulled the door handle, just enough that the light inside the car came on. Then someone thumped on my window.

"Belle!" Justin waved. He was dressed normally,

but he had these huge furry mittens on his hands, like animal paws.

I was so relieved to see him I burst out laughing.

"Is this Justin of the awesomesauce costume?" Mom asked.

I nodded.

"You coming or what?" Justin called to me through the window.

I turned to my mom. "You promise? You'll answer the phone when I call? And you'll come right back to get me?"

"Yes, Zu."

"And you won't stop anywhere between here and home? So if I call you after five minutes, you'll be home by the phone?"

"I promise."

Three hundred seconds.

I took a deep breath. Clutching my mom's phone in my left hand, I stepped out of the car.

"What are you?" Justin asked, looking at my Red Sox cap. "A baseball player?"

I shut the door and watched my mom's car pull

away from the curb. I swallowed hard and then looked at him.

"Just a regular guy," I said. "Can't a regular guy be a hero?"

"Hmm..." He stroked his chin with his furry paw. "Doesn't happen often, but I suppose it can happen now and then."

I heard the music start inside the building, some song I didn't know. But apparently other kids did, because a bunch of kids cheered and rushed toward the door.

"Hey," Justin said, pointing to the parking lot. "There's Mrs. Turton." He waved his furry mitts like a crazy man. "Hey, Mrs. Turton!"

Mrs. Turton wore silver sparkle sneakers, which I thought was funny. "What are you dressed as, Mrs. Turton?" Justin asked.

She unzipped her coat, placed her hands on her hips, and stood with her chin thrust upward, superhero-style. Beneath her coat, she wore a T-shirt that read I TEACH SCIENCE. WHAT'S YOUR SUPER-POWER?

"And you, Mr. Maloney?" she asked. "Are you a werewolf?"

"Nope," Justin said. "But I'll bet Belle here knows what I am."

"Yeah, I know what you are," I said.

They both waited.

"He's the Beast," I said. Justin beamed.

"Ah," Mrs. Turton said. "Well, I hope the Beast is ready to boogie, because Mrs. Turton is ready to dance. Look," she added, wiggling one of her sneakers in the air. "I've even got my dancing shoes on."

Justin and Mrs. Turton walked toward the front doors. When Mrs. Turton opened one of the doors, loud music spilling outside, Justin turned back to me.

"Come on, Belle," he said.

I imagined the scene inside the gym—circles of kids, hopping up and down to the beat. All those costumes. All that noise and motion.

"I need to make a phone call first," I said.

I turned away from the entrance. I counted to three hundred.

Three hundred seconds, which was 1,380 new jellyfish stings.

Then I dialed. I pressed the phone to my ear.

"Hello?" said the voice on the other end of the line.

"Dad," I said.

I probably hadn't said that word—*Dad*—in over five months. Five months, which is 150 days, which is millions and millions of seconds, but I couldn't calculate exactly how many right then.

There was a long silence, as if he honestly didn't know who was calling.

"I was just thinking," I said. I bit my lip. "Maybe we should go see those dinosaur tracks."

When Dad finally answered, his voice sounded funny, like it had cracked a little.

"Okay," he said.

From inside the building, the song changed. I knew this one. It was from a few years ago, back when Franny and I were friends and I never imagined it would be any other way.

"I want Aaron to come, too," I said.

"Yeah," Dad said. "Of course. Of course Aaron can come."

"And Rocco."

"Yeah. I'll call them to arrange it, honey."

I leaned against the brick exterior of the Eugene Field Memorial Middle School and listened to the music coming from inside the gym.

"Anything else, Suzy?"

"No," I said. "Not now."

Pause. "I'm really glad you called, Suzy."

"Okay."

"I'll see you tomorrow?"

"Yeah."

"Same time, same place, right?"

I imagined our pink vinyl booth at Ming Palace, the fish tank and those fish that saw only their own reflections. I thought about all those nights Dad and I had spent never saying a single word.

"I don't know," I said. "Maybe we can try someplace new tomorrow."

It was his turn to pause.

"Yeah. Wherever you want, Suzy."

"Okay."

"Okay."

And then suddenly it seemed sort of embarrassing, because I was finally talking, but I couldn't actually think of anything else to say.

"Bye, Dad."

"Goodbye, sweetie." I could barely hear him.

There was a click, and then he was gone.

I felt a tap on my shoulder. I turned around, expecting to see Justin. But it wasn't Justin. It was Sarah Johnston.

"Hey, Suzy," she said. Sarah was dressed like a ninja, all in black. "Have you been inside yet?"

I shook my head.

"I just got here, too," she said. She paused, then added, "I've never been to a dance, have you?"

I shook my head again.

"We could go in together," she said. She looked nervous. Maybe even…hopeful. Then she added, almost apologetically, "I still don't really know a lot of people here. I guess I'd rather not go in alone."

I was so surprised I didn't even think about my words. "But you have so many friends," I said.

She was Aubrey's lab partner. I'd seen her talking to Molly. I'd seen her shirt knotted up at the waist like the others'.

"Not really," she said. "I mean, I know kids, but it's not like I have *friends*."

Sarah Johnston, who did her science paper on zombie ants because they had scared her.

Sarah Johnston, who had lingered to watch the video in Mrs. Turton's office.

Sarah Johnston, who, if I had to be honest, seemed pretty okay, actually.

"Mrs. Turton is in there," I said. "I think she and Justin Maloney are dancing together."

Sarah smiled. "Remember when Mrs. Turton dressed up like Albert Einstein?"

I laughed.

"She's my favorite teacher," said Sarah.

"Yeah," I agreed. "Mine, too."

That's when I had this thought: If Mrs. Turton was right, if we each had 20 billion of Shakespeare's atoms in us, and Shakespeare lived four hundred years ago all the way across an ocean, then we must have Franny's atoms in us, too. And way more than Shakespeare's—I mean, Franny had been with us, breathing and walking and eating and laughing, and shedding skin. She'd been a part of us, every day for a long, long time.

Suddenly I imagined the universe as a giant set of LEGOs, all those pieces constructing endless forms, then coming apart only to create new forms.

Sarah and I walked into the building together, then paused at the entrance of the gym. It was dark and hung with streamers. Different-colored lights circled all around the room, specks of light traveling over the floor and walls and ceilings, and right over kids' faces. If I squinted just right, I could see only the lights, flashing and moving like stars in an empty sky.

I opened my eyes and saw a gym full of kids. Then I squinted again and the lights became underwater creatures, flashing their bioluminescence, all those underwater signals, at one another.

I imagined floating up to the ceiling of the gym and looking down at all those different groups, dancing in their tight circles. I imagined how each circle would look as it moved in time to the beat, all those arms and legs moving out and in at exactly the same moment. Each group might look like a heart beating, maybe.

Or a jellyfish pulsing.

"There's Justin and Mrs. Turton," Sarah said. She pointed.

Even from this distance, I could see that Justin's face was already sweaty. His head was tossed back; he was laughing. All the kids in their group clasped their hands together, moving their arms in a circle like they were churning butter. As if he could sense me staring, Justin looked up and waved.

I squinted, and he disappeared into sea and sky.

"You want to go over?" Sarah asked.

My mom's phone was still in my hand.

Maybe it was because of the pulsing. Or maybe it was as simple as Justin's wave, or Sarah's smile, or the way Mrs. Turton moved her hands in sync with the kids.

But I stopped squinting. I placed my mom's phone in my shirt pocket, next to the photo of Aaron. I took a deep breath.

"Yeah," I said to Sarah. "Let's go."

author's note

Although most of the characters in this book are fictional, the jellyfish experts, including Jamie Seymour, are real. I've done my best to honor their work and their achievements by representing them as factually as possible. There is one very big exception: Diana Nyad's historic Cuba-Florida swim, her fifth attempt, actually took place on Monday, September 2, 2013. I considered fictionalizing her character, as well as those of the other researchers, rather than misrepresent the date of her swim. In the end, though, I decided not to do that. Nyad's swim was a profoundly impressive feat. She showed grit, tenacity, and strength, and she deserves full recognition for the accomplishment, even if the date didn't fit neatly into the time line of Suzy's story.

New Englanders will recognize the touch tank, jellies exhibit, and giant ocean tank described in the early chapters as being part of the experience at the New England Aquarium in Boston, although the jellies exhibit does not specifically discuss the Irukandji.

The photographs Mrs. Turton refers to in class include *Earthrise*, which was taken by astronaut William Anders in 1968 during the *Apollo 8* mission; and *Pale Blue Dot*, which was taken in 1990, at a distance of 3.7 billion miles, by the *Voyager 1* space probe, a spacecraft that has traveled all that distance using less computing power than an iPhone. Mrs. Turton's words about that photograph echo those of the late Carl Sagan—astronomer and humanist—in his book *Pale Blue Dot: A Vision of the Human Future in Space*.

The book upon which Suzy reflects in the chapter "How to Not Say Something Important" is Kate DiCamillo's *Because of Winn-Dixie*.

The video Suzy and Justin watch in the "Pollination" chapter is presented in filmmaker Louie Schwartzberg's TED Talk "The Hidden Beauty of Pollination," which you can see on TED.com.

The "Most Astounding Fact" video was made by videographer Max Schlickenmeyer. He combines a quote from the delightful Neil DeGrasse Tyson with images taken by the Hubble Space Telescope and other images from space. DeGrasse Tyson gave the quote to *Time* magazine in 2012, in response to the question "What is the most astounding fact you can share with us about the universe?"

If you enjoy thinking about the universe, consider picking up a copy of Bill Bryson's *A Really Short History of Nearly Everything* (Delacorte Books for Young Readers, 2009), which is a kid-friendly version of a longer adult book. Bryson explains the origins of the universe, the natural history of our planet, and the astonishing fact of our own existence.

If you want to marvel at jellyfish and other alien creatures of the sea, you will surely adore Claire Nouvian's *The Deep: The Extraordinary Creatures of the Abyss* (University of Chicago Press, 2007). It is an adult photography book, but the world it showcases is bizarre and fascinating for people of all ages.

acknowledgments

This story was born from a failure. A few years ago, I became captivated by jellyfish—about what they tell us about ourselves and also about our planet. I poured everything I had into a nonfiction essay about the animals, which I submitted with great hopes to a glossy magazine. The editors said they were quite interested. Then they held on to it for a year...and ultimately rejected it.

I wasn't ready to let go of jellyfish. Much like Suzy, I began researching jellyfish experts and taking notes, not quite sure where my efforts would take me. This is the story that emerged.

It's true what Mrs. Turton says: We do learn more from our failures than from our successes.

I'm tremendously grateful to my agent and friend Mollie Glick of Foundry Literary and Media, for both her whip-smart editorial feedback and her savvy in helping this book find the right home. Thanks, too, to Foundry's Emily Brown, a sharp-eyed reader and a darned hard worker; to Jessica Regel, who helped bring the book to an audience around the world; and to Joy Fowlkes.

Andrea Spooner—perhaps because she'd once slept for a period of weeks with an article about the immortal jellyfish by her bedside—gamely took a risk on a strange manuscript about an oddball kid who's obsessed with an alien creature. She *got* it. Then she guided it deftly and meticulously. Thanks, too, to the entire team at Little Brown Books for Young Readers, especially Deirdre Jones, Russell Busse, Victoria Stapleton, and Megan Tingley.

Neil Gaiman once said, "Google can bring you back 100,000 answers; a librarian can bring you back the right one." Thanks to Kirsten Rose and Helen Olshever for always bringing me back the right one, no matter what I asked. Meanwhile, Elinor Goodwin at the Print Shop of Williamstown printed out about eight million drafts for me. Thanks to fact-checker Christopher Berendes, copy editor Barbara Perris, and my friend Jeffrey Thomas, MD, PhD, for his scientific insights and inspiration, as well as his unflagging support.

I'm grateful to the kids at Pine Cobble School, especially the members of writing club, for reminding me how wise and compassionate kids can be...and also for their hilarity and all-around awesomeness. Please continue being real and true and thoughtful and curious as you make your way through this complicated world.

And a huge thank-you to teachers everywhere... including all my own.

I've been blessed with many great friends, among them Janine Hetherington, my best reader; Molly Kerns, my most enthusiastic cheerleader; and Rebeccah Kamp, the reigning queen of quietly helping others when they need it.

Thanks to all of my family for being in my corner, always.

And the biggest thank-you of all goes to the three people with whom I share my every day: to Blair, whose steady, supportive presence is proof that marrying him remains the least *cray cray* decision I've ever made; to Merrie, who reminds me that life, and books, should always be an adventure; and to Charlotte, whose curiosity has opened me up to countless hidden wonders of this world. I love you people.

about the author

Ali Benjamin grew up outside New York City, in a rickety old house that neighbors thought was haunted. As a child she spent countless hours catching bugs and frogs; *The Thing About Jellyfish* emerged from her fascination with the natural world. She is the cowriter of HIV-positive teen Paige Rawl's coming-of-age memoir *Positive*, as well as Tim Howard's *New York Times* bestseller *The Keeper*. She is a member of New England Science Writers. She lives in rural Massachusetts with her husband, two kids, and Australian shepherd named Mollie.